PATRICIA PENROSE

Death on the Night Riviera

D1519882

I dedicate this novel to my family. I appreciate their unfailing support. And a special thanks to those poor souls (you know who you are) that read my humble scribbles time and again and offer feedback and encouragement. Thank you so much.

Contents

Mrs. Crumpet's Peachy

London, May 1916

I knocked on the front door. It opened a tad, then jerked to a halt, held fast by a bulky metal chain. A "V" of light spilled out and illuminated an eyeball framed in delicate wrinkles, a slice of gaudy plaid bathrobe, and the toe of one dainty pink slipper. "Mrs. Crumpet? It is Alberta. I'm on blackout inspection tonight and must caution you your sitting room light is showing again."

"Oh, Alberta dear, I'm so sorry," the elderly voice shook, "but please, could you come in? I desperately need your help; it's Peachy again." The sweet, dithery little woman stepped back and slammed the door in my face. The knob quivered, and the chain clanked and rattled.

1

"Remember your hall light," I called through the solid wood. The door opened, and I stepped into a dim, tiny vestibule. The scent of wintergreen liniment and cinnamon enveloped me. I closed the door and leaned against it. Mrs. Crumpet, standing on tiptoe like an aged ballerina, turned the gaslight back up.

"I'm sorry, dear, about the lights, but I've been so frantic about Peachy. She disappeared two days ago during the last air raid bell. You know how loud noises drive her crazy."

"Two days, that's not like her." I sat on a rickety chair with a groan, glad to rest my feet. "What happened, exactly?"

"That mean Martin Goolsby was on duty. He pounded on my door and yelled, 'lights out!' I opened the door to give him a scold, and Peachy ran between our legs and down the street, howling like a mad thing." The older woman's hand gripped mine, "Mr. Goolsby hates Peachy. Alberta, you can search while you do your rounds, can't you?"

"Yes, of course, I'll keep an eye out for her." I shook my finger, "On one condition, keep your curtains drawn. Any bit of light can be a beacon for a zeppelin. For everyone's sake, we must be careful." I took Mrs. Crumpet's frail, blue-veined hand in mine to soften my words.

"You are such a dear girl." She patted my hand, then stood and gestured to the sitting room. "Now, come fix my curtain."

I smiled and shook my head as I followed the elderly woman down the narrow hallway. I weaved between the fragile whatnot cupboard (the one that held prized souvenir cups and saucers from Brighton and Torquay) and the three-foot-tall, blue and white china vase full of peacock feathers. Then I brushed past a ghastly table made of an elephant's foot that Colonel Crumpet brought home from India years ago. I plucked the edge of the heavy cretonne curtain and gave it a sharp shake to smooth it

2

tight against the window frame.

"There you are. Maybe you should just keep these curtains drawn."

"Oh, I usually do."

I had a fleeting thought that a correlation existed between that open curtain and occasions when sweet old Mrs. Crumpet needed help. I opened my mouth to comment but noticed the gleam of unshed tears in her eyes. I changed my mind. "Well, I must be off. Mr. Wickham is working the next street. I'll ask him to pass the word along about Peachy." I straightened my helmet, double-checked my torch, and then gave the elderly woman an encouraging pat on her frail shoulder.

"Tell the vicar hello," she said with a flutter of fingers.

With a lift of my hand, I nodded and stepped carefully down the stairs and out into the damp spring night. I picked my way along Pickering Street past blocks of upper-middle-class row houses, which slumbered, solid, and respectable, and checked for blackout infractions. I also kept a sharp eye out for one obese, white English bulldog named Peachy. Instead, I spotted the middle-aged, bowlegged form of Ralph Wickham, my inspection partner. I flashed my torch and then crossed the street to meet him. "All clear here, Ralph, although I did have to speak to Mrs. Crumpet again."

Ralph shook his head. "Sometimes I think those old ladies 'show light' on purpose just to have a visitor. Mrs. Bennett, over on Bland Street, used to do that a couple times a week, just so's I'd stop in for tea."

"And what did you do?"

Ralph started to chuckle. "I'd go step in some mud and get my shoes nice and covered, see? Then I'd walk through her parlor to close the curtains. After a couple of visits like that, she kept her drapes closed tight."

"Oh, you," I gave him a quick elbow to the ribs, "I never believe a single thing you say." We walked for a few minutes in companionable silence, then I spoke. "Mrs. Crumpet told me Peachy has run away again. Seems Martin Goolsby gave her a warning on Monday, and the dog slipped through the door."

"It wouldn't surprise me if Goolsby murdered that dog. He hates that animal. Every time Peachy gets near Martin Goolsby, the dog grabs Martin's pant leg and won't let go. One day I saw Goolsby walk down the pavement, cussing, dragging that dog behind him, trying to shake her off. Funniest thing you ever saw."

"Did that happen Monday?"

"Naw, this was a few weeks back. I haven't worked with Martin since."

"Why would Peachy behave that way? I never have trouble with her."

"Mrs. Crumpet told me Peachy hates certain men. I've never had a problem with the pup, either. But then, who wouldn't love me?" said Ralph.

"That's true," I said as I slipped my arm through his.

We reached the edge of St. Hugh's churchyard a few moments later. Ralph paused, "Ah, here's where I leave you, ma' dear. Give my best to Vicar Holdaway."

"I will. You'll keep on the lookout for Peachy?"

"Of course," Ralph winked, "anything for Mrs. Crumpet."

"Thanks, good night Ralph."

Ralph and I parted ways. He crossed the street and turned the corner at Froggatt's Park, and I followed the black wrought-iron fence that encircled St. Hugh's graveyard.

The Vicar of St. Hugh's

The graveyard was a welcome sight; it meant I was almost home. On a childish impulse, I put the tip of my umbrella between the arrow-shaped fence staves surrounding the cemetery and quickened my pace. The contact of metal upon metal produced a raucous clickety-clack that was loud enough to wake the dead. Thank goodness there was no one close enough to hear. The only buildings on this block were the old stone church of St. Hugh's and my home, the Vicarage, which sat in its shadow.

The Vicarage was a hodge-podge of styles. The original stone block structure, built in 1690, was a plain, square, two-storied building with two chimneys and a dark gray slate roof. In 1896, the wide porch and a new kitchen wing were added. I let myself into the front hallway and heaved a sigh of relief. I unlaced my serviceable boots and took off the clunky metal helmet. Then shrugged off my Red Cross Voluntary Aid Detachment jacket and hung them, along with my umbrella, on the hall tree below an old wavy mirror. I sat on the bench, usually full of waiting parishioners, and tugged off my boots. It was heaven to pad in stocking feet to the kitchen. I stooped to open the door of the ancient enamel stove and used the poker to coax the smoldering bits of coal into a heat-producing flame. Within minutes, the teakettle whistled, and the Blue Willow teapot had warmed. I dumped the water out, scooped just the right amount of tea leaves in, filled it from the boiling kettle, and set it on the kitchen table to steep. I was just about to relax and pour myself a nice strong cup of the amber brew when there was a timid knock at the front door.

"Oh, piffle," I muttered and padded to the front hall. The moonlight threw a man's shadow on the opaque glass. With a groan, I slipped some old shoes on, heels protruding, and opened the door.

"Yes…, oh it's you, Mr. Goolsby. Can I help you?"

Martin Goolsby's eyes darted quickly to my face. A slow flush spread as he whisked off his hat, exposing the glistening greasiness of his black hair. The young man's gaze could not hold mine for more than a second; in acute discomfort, he looked at the cap in his hands and mumbled, "I h-h-have an appointment with Reverend H-Holdaway."

"I'm sorry, Mr. Goolsby, but it's late. Father cannot see you this evening. I'm sure he'll get in touch with you tomorrow. I'll tell him you were here." I gave a slight smile and stepped back. I had almost shut the door when I remembered Peachy. "Oh, Martin," the young man lifted his head expectantly, "have you seen Mrs. Crumpet's Peachy?"

Martin's face suffused with red, and his eyes narrowed. "What makes you think I'd know somethin' about that animal?"

I stood there with my mouth open, shocked by his response.

"Miss Alberta," Martin Goolsby continued, lifting his head, "I do know somethin' else, though," he paused.

I just stood there; I refused to take the bait and ask what. I began to close the door.

He raised his voice and continued, "Your father will be leaving soon." I stopped, frozen. The corners of Mr. Goolsby's mouth turned up into a smirk. "My mother and me will be living here."

"Pardon me, what did you say?"

"Are you hard of hearing?" Goolsby said a little louder and stepped closer, "My mother and me will move in here to help the new vicar. He'll be coming in a few weeks. I need to speak to Vicar Holdaway to get things settled."

I stood in the doorway, stunned, "And how in the world can you know that?"

"I know a lot of things," said Goolsby, grinning and nodding his head.

My hand itched to slap the smirk off his greasy face. However, I tightened my grip on the door frame. I stepped backward into the Vicarage hallway and gave the door a satisfying glass-rattling slam. I stood in a daze for a moment, then sat on the hall bench with a jolt. "Father," I called. There was no answer; the house was silent. "Father," I walked down the dark hall and opened the door to the study. In the dim light, I saw him; face down on the large mahogany desk in the center of the room. I crept in and turned up the gaslight.

I bent over Father's lightly snoring form; the acrid fumes of Napoleon brandy assailed me. I moved nearer and saw the crumpled paper. The letter, written in a fine hand on linen stationery, was from the Bishop of the Anglican Church. I read it. Father's request had met with refusal again. The previous letters and been vague and kind, but in this reply, the Bishop was painfully clear, ". . . too unstable to withstand the rigors of the front or the chaplaincy in any capacity." The letter said, "Vicar Holdaway is granted a leave of absence."

Tears welled up in my eyes, "Oh, God." I crossed to the window seat and picked up the plaid wool blanket Mrs. Pewter always kept there. With the itchy cloth clutched to my chest, I walked over to Father's unconscious form. I lay the blanket gently upon him, touched his shoulder lightly for comfort, and then tiptoed out, leaving the Vicar of St. Hugh's snoring in peace.

The Vicar's Decision

I lingered longer than usual the next morning over my ablutions. Faraway clinks and rattles indicated Mrs. Pewter was busy about her business downstairs. Then came enticing smells of coffee and bacon, which meant breakfast was ready, and I could put off facing Father no longer.

I put my night things under my pillow. The blue chenille spread was soft and nubby under my palms as I smoothed the bedclothes. Everything was so familiar; hard to believe we might leave this place soon. With a sigh, I stood, straightened my shoulders, and walked out the door. I stepped down the creaky stairs and paused to peer out the small diamond-shaped stained glass window. The four panes - yellow, red, blue, and green, made the backyard seem like a fairyland but still allowed for a brief check of the weather. This May had been unseasonably wet and cool. Now foggy mist floated from the ground as the sun's rays struggled to touch and warm the earth.

A strangled gasp from below made me start. I turned to see our housekeeper at the foot of the stairs. Mrs. Pewter's hand flew to her chest; she closed her eyes and gripped the banister for support. "Oh my land, I thought you were your mother. She used to stand there looking out that window, and with the light from the red glass shining on your hair, you look so like her."

I stepped down, and the titan locks turned back to nutmeg brown. "I wish I had Mother's flaming red hair. It was glorious." I reached out and put my arm around the broad shoulders of the housekeeper.

"It was that," said Mrs. Pewter. "Sorry to be so fanciful, I'm just being sentimental today."

I followed Mrs. Pewter into the dining room. She headed through the swinging door to the kitchen, and I pulled out the pressed-back dining chair, making a purposeful screech to announce my arrival. Instead of Father's familiar grin, I faced a solid wall of the *London Times*. The newspaper gave a wiggle as pages turned but did not fall. I put my elbows on the table and waited. After a few minutes, I rolled my eyes, stood, reached across, and pulled down the center of the newspaper. Two very bloodshot eyes and a very sheepish grin greeted me.

"Hoped you'd be a sport and let me suffer in silence," said Father.

"No, I will not let you suffer in silence. We need to discuss this. I read the Bishop's letter."

"Now, Alberta, you must have some respect for my age if not for my position or behavior." Father folded the newspaper and set it on the table. "Glad you came in, though; this war news depresses me."

It relieved me to see some of the old sparkle in his eyes. "We really do need to discuss that letter."

Just then, Mrs. Pewter came in carrying coffee and something grainy and brown that resembled toast. Father raised his hand,

10

"Pas devant la domestique."

"Well, you can go right ahead and talk in front of this 'domestique' 'cause I bet I know more than you do," said Mrs. Pewter as she set the coffeepot and toast rack on the table. "That detestable Goolsby woman got wind of the Bishop's letter somehow and has you and Miss Alberta packed and out of here already, with herself installed as housekeeper. She couldn't wait to let me know!" Mrs. Pewter turned on her heel, clutched the serving tray to her ample bosom, and headed for the kitchen.

"What? That's why that squirmy son of hers came to see you last night."

"Well, if the news is all about the town, I may as well accept defeat and scamper off to safety."

Mrs. Pewter stopped dead. "Now that's no way to talk, Vicar Holdaway. Shame on you. You don't need to be at the Front; there's as much to do for the soldiers after they come home." Mrs. Pewter jabbed her finger on the newspaper. "Says so right here. Our boys are coming home with more than physical wounds. You have a rare gift with such things."

"But Mrs. Pewter, how can I counsel others about what I'm unsure of myself?"

"Did you see the article on the little village that lost twenty-three boys at once because they were all friends and relatives who joined up in one of those Buddy Battalions? You think you would have no comfort to offer those families?"

"Mrs. Pewter's right, as usual," I said, picking up my napkin and laying it on my lap. "I need a cup of coffee, you, Father?"

"Yes, please, dear." Father sat straighter and turned to the housekeeper. "Thank you, Mrs. Pewter. That was a fine sermon; I'll take it under advisement. I suspect you are quite right, and I am heartily ashamed."

Mrs. Pewter smiled and patted the vicar's shoulder. "I'll have your breakfast out in a jiffy, sir. Drink your coffee."

Mrs. Pewter came in a few minutes later with two plates heaped with fried potatoes and just a wisp of bacon on the side. The vicar laid his snowy white napkin on his lap and rubbed his hands together in anticipation. "Aw, Mrs. Pewter, you're an angel. I feel better already." The housekeeper moved quickly to hide the smile on her face. She caught my eye and winked.

After breakfast, Father and I went to his study. Mrs. Pewter had cleared away all traces of last night's episode. The curtains were open wide, and a bright patch of sun highlighted the key pattern on the red Turkish carpet. Father still had a sheepish and embarrassed look on his face. "Alberta, I'm so very sorry."

"I know, Father, we needn't discuss last night. However, what do you propose to do about the Bishop's request? Can you leave St. Hugh's?"

"It isn't a request, my dear, and maybe it's time to leave this place. I have floundered since your mother died. She bore so much of the emotional burden of my ministry here. All the families of this parish have lost so much in this first year of the war, and I can't seem to help them anymore; maybe I never could."

Father sighed and turned his chair to look out the window. "The other day, a woman came to me and asked me to pray for the repose of her son's soul. The Anglican Church forbids that practice, but how could I refuse to give that small comfort? I am frequently at odds with my superiors these days, it seems. That is why I apply for the Chaplaincy time after time. I want to do something to really help."

"We all feel guilt at being safe at home, Father. For instance, my Red Cross clerical work and fundraising. That is hardly the work I thought I would do, but it's necessary just the same."

Father faced me and opened his top desk drawer. He took out a leaflet. "Look at this, Alberta, the latest *Bishop's Bulletin*. It is all about the evils of alcohol." I took the church pamphlet from his trembling hand. "This is what I am supposed to build this month's sermons upon. Maybe you should get your Brownie camera and take a photo of me sprawled senseless on this desk. That would be the perfect object lesson." Father held up his hand, "No, say nothing; I know I'm an ungrateful whiner, and I despise myself."

"So what are we going to do?"

"You, my dear, are staying here. You can room with Binky, can't you? Mrs. Pewter could stay with her sister. Just until I sort myself out." Father rubbed his temples. "A few nights ago, I heard and saw something; a hallucination, possibly. I have no choice but to leave and take myself in hand. I'll go to Highdrift."

"Highdrift? I thought the house was abandoned."

"Your mother and I went down there while you were abroad, just after she inherited Highdrift from Uncle James. We had a few necessary repairs made and were trying to decide what to do with it when your mother became ill."

"But Cornwall, that's so far away," I said.

"Only a night's train journey," Father said as he patted my hand.

Grimwood Mausoleum

"It's only a night's train journey, Father said. I almost broke down and cried at the look on his face. It is so unlike him to give up on anything or anyone."

I sat at the kitchen table with Mrs. Pewter. She reached her rough hand across the table and covered mine. "I have no problem taking some time off. My sister, Nancy, wants to set up her house to take in borders and needs some help, but what about you?"

"Father's not going to Highdrift alone, that's for sure. I don't care what he says."

"Good girl, I don't think your Father should be by himself."

"I agree. He told me he thinks he is imagining things, which concerns me. Did Father mention seeing anything the night before last?"

Mrs. Pewter squeezed my hand with a sharp intake of breath. "Your Father noticed something odd too?"

"What do you mean, too?"

Mrs. Pewter put a hand to her heart. "I'm so relieved. I saw something in the graveyard. Everything was so dim with the blackout and all; I thought it must be my imagination. But maybe not if the vicar saw something too."

"Well, what did you see?" I asked.

"Spring-heeled Jack," said the solid and sober Mrs. Pewter.

"A what, did you say?"

"Not a what, I guess it would be more of a 'who'; Spring-heeled Jack."

"Who in the world is Spring-heeled Jack?"

"Oh, he was in all the newspapers years ago. We were all terrified of a creature that leaped, bounded, and had glowing eyes. The newspapers dubbed him *Spring-heeled Jack* because of the way he moved. He haunted parks and graveyards."

"And you saw that in the graveyard last night?"

"Well, probably not," Mrs. Pewter said, her cheeks turning bright pink. "But I saw something with glowing eyes that jiggled."

"That jiggled? Well, thank goodness there was no leaping and bounding!" I couldn't help myself; I put a hand over my mouth. I caught Mrs. Pewter's eye as she let out a big guffaw. Mrs. Pewter shook hard with laughter. She grabbed her sides and tried to catch her breath. I had tears running down my cheeks.

"What is going on here?" Father said as he stepped through the kitchen door, eyes wide with surprise.

I looked at Father and tried to speak. "Mrs. Pewter s-saw," I dissolved into laughter again. Mrs. Pewter, head on the table, gasped for breath.

Father lifted the teapot's lid and set it gently on the pristine tablecloth. He picked up the Blue Willow pot, lifted it to his nose, sniffed, and then raised his eyebrows. "I thought maybe you filled this with some of my brandy," he shook his head, "but

15

it's only tea."

I took a few deep gulps of air and dabbed at my damp eyes with a napkin. "Oh my, that hurt. I was trying to tell you that Mrs. Pewter and I were discussing what she saw in the graveyard."

"You mean I wasn't hallucinating? I did see something?"

I nodded, "Seems you both saw something."

Father pulled out a chair and sat down, letting out a *whoosh* of relief. "Thank God. You can't know how much better that makes me feel. What exactly did you see, Mrs. Pewter?"

"That's what I was telling Alberta before she made me laugh. I saw glowing eyes moving up and down in the old abandoned cemetery. I know that sounds ridiculous."

"Not to me," Father said.

"I think I'll go out there and look around." I jumped up from the table like a Jack-in-the-box. "Where exactly did you see whatever you saw?"

"I had just turned the corner and was heading towards Pickering Street; I crossed over to Froggatt's Park and saw a glint out of the corner of my eye. I stepped closer to the fence to look through the spokes and saw movement around the old graveyard," Mrs. Pewter said.

I left the kitchen, went to the hall closet, pulled out my oldest coat, cinched its belt tight around my waist, and picked up my trusty umbrella. After patting my coat to assure myself that my torch was in my pocket, I opened the door and stepped out onto the front porch. The morning sun had disappeared; it was chilly and damp. The thick atmospheric fog made me shiver.

As I closed the door, I felt a sharp tug; Father and Mrs. Pewter stepped out. Mrs. Pewter brushed past. "I saw whatever I saw over this way."

16

The three of us headed up the walkway. Within seconds misty droplets of water covered Mrs. Pewter's iron-gray bun like a net of seed pearls, and I could feel the moisture seeping through my ankle-length skirt. The housekeeper led the way around the shiny black cemetery fence where each fence stave resembled an arrow pointing toward heaven. The monuments and stones in the "new" cemetery (circa 1750) were free of lichen and lovingly festooned with spring bouquets. This contrasted sharply with the aura of the "old" graveyard.

Single file, we crossed the street. The closer we got to the old abandoned cemetery, the faster my pulse raced. The fence was high and rusted; a padlocked gate barred our way. Beyond that gate was a mass of unkempt trees and shrubs. Vines and waist-high grass obliterated stone crosses and other monuments to the dead that tilted at drunken angles.

"We may need a key," Father said as he bent down and rattled the chain and padlock.

"No, look," I pointed to the muddy ground. "The gate has been dragged; there's a trench here." Mrs. Pewter stepped back as Father, and I inspected the gate itself. "The hinge pins are gone," I said. Father lifted and pulled. The gate moved back with an ear-splitting screech and then listed to one side.

"You know, I think I heard that screech. That's what roused me the other night and drew me to the window," Father said. "And then I heard an echoing howl."

"An echoing howl and jiggling eyes; this keeps getting worse," I said as I stepped around the gate. The three of us squelched through the mud until we found solid footing.

"There is a central pathway here under this tall grass. We should try to follow this as far as we can," Father whispered.

A light breeze came up, and the sun pierced the cloud cover

as we carefully picked our way across the lonely graveyard. Mrs. Pewter stopped and pointed. "I saw some light and those glowing eyes between those columns."

"That's the entrance to the Grimwood Mausoleum," Father murmured.

Mrs. Pewter's eyes widened. A hard lump formed in my throat. We continued our deliberate pace, heads down, watching our feet as we pushed through the tangle of ivy and creeping buttercup that cluttered the path. The amount of undergrowth and tree cover increased as we neared the massive granite pillars. A riotous net of bramble, nettle, ivy, and morning glory ran up the sides, over the flat roof, and covered the mausoleum. "Look at the front; the weeds seem to have been cut back recently."

"That's odd," Father said. "Why would anyone take the trouble to move that gate and cut down these vines? Who knows this place even exists anymore?"

"Someone with something to hide, obviously," I said. "Or maybe someone wanted a private air raid shelter?"

"I doubt anyone would want to shelter here," said Mrs. Pewter. "There's an old story that this was a Plague Pit."

"It's not just a story, I'm afraid," Father said as he held back a particularly nasty bramble vine. "This cemetery was on the outskirts of London in 1665 when the plague struck. Grimwood was one of many emergency burial sites."

As we drew closer to the mausoleum, I could make out the two Doric columns. Above the columns was a frieze inscribed with the name Grimwood. An apt name for this distressing place. As we crept up to the granite tomb, I noticed the pockmarked texture of the old stone. The odor of rot and mildew permeated the damp air and clung to my skin. The same mildew and

18

dampness weakened the wood planks that blocked the original entryway.

I stopped and pointed, "Look, a few of these planks are removed." I reached down with the tip of my umbrella and swung the outermost board to the left. I repeated the procedure with the next plank. I pulled my torch from my pocket, wrapped my coat tightly around my legs, and knelt. I shone the light through the small opening. Its meager glow showed only leaves and twigs scattered about the stone floor. "We'll have to take the planks off; I can only see a few yards." I snapped off the torch and stood.

"Here, if we swing a couple more boards over, I can crawl in," Father said.

"Maybe it would be better to. . . ," Mrs. Pewter stopped with a quick intake of breath. "What was that?"

"It came from inside. It sounded like a whimper." I felt cold chills and then a rush of adrenaline. Father and I pried off boards. Mrs. Pewter dragged the planks out of the way.

In a few minutes, we had a narrow entryway. I started forward; Father touched my arm. "Alberta, let me." He gently took the torch from my hand. "Just stay put till I give the 'All Clear.'" Father stuck his head through the gap and barely squeezed through the opening. His clothes snagged on the rough, splintery wood, but he made it inside and then flicked on the torch.

"What do you see?" I asked.

"Well, someone has definitely been in here. There are muddy tracks on the floor and piles of leaves in the corners," Father's voice echoed.

"Are there actual footprints?"

"Let me see…, um, looks like a shoe about my size and *yeow*,"

Father yelled. A shaky laugh followed.

"What, what is it?" Mrs. Pewter and I screamed.

"Just a rat," Father's voice echoed.

"A ra...," I screamed as I saw the large, greasy, hunched-back rat come out of the mausoleum. His long, naked, scaly tail went over the toe of my boot. I jumped back in disgust and bumped into Mrs. Pewter. I knocked the poor woman onto the rough stone path, and she just sat there, frozen, with her mouth in a big "O." We watched the rodent scuttle closer to her. Then Mrs. Pewter panicked and scooted backward along the walkway, just ahead of the squeaking rodent.

I ran towards Mrs. Pewter, opening and closing my umbrella like a bellow, and screamed like a maniac. At first, I seemed to herd the vermin directly towards the safety of the housekeeper's voluminous skirt. I quickly changed to a more southerly course, and the rodent veered off to seek the security of the nearby bramble patch.

I reached my hand out, and Mrs. Pewter grabbed it like a lifeline. I helped her stand; we brushed moss and leaves off her brown serge skirt. "Are you all right?"

Mrs. Pewter shivered as she put her hand to her heart. "My word, I've never been so scared. I'm terrified of rats."

"Alberta!" Father called.

I patted Mrs. Pewter's hand, "I'll be right back."

"No, I'm coming too," Mrs. Pewter said with a quiver.

I led her to the doorway. "In you go then; I'll follow." Mrs. Pewter slid in slowly. I went close behind. "Brrr, it's chilly in here," I said as I turned around in the dank, somber chamber, "and it has an odd smell." I heard a whimper, then a whine. In the far corner sat a massive pile of leaves; a hazy white lump was buried underneath them. The pile of leaves heaved. Mrs.

Pewter let out a scream that bounced off the solid granite walls. The white blob under the leaves let out a weak growl. "Peachy, Peachy honey," leaves bobbed up and down, crunched, and crackled as Peachy wagged her stubby tail. I ran to the corner, knelt on the deathly cold stone floor, reached into the damp clumps of rotted leaves, and felt Peachy's chilled body. After brushing the poor dog off, she lifted her head for a moment and laid it back down. Her large round body relaxed with a deep sigh, and she closed her bulging eyes.

"Is she dead?" said Mrs. Pewter.

I placed my hand on Peachy's body and gauged its rhythmic rise and fall. "She's not dead but suffering from exposure, I'd guess." Peachy shivered. I slipped off my raincoat, covered the dog with it, and tucked it underneath.

Father's hand touched my shoulder, "Here, Alberta, let me." Father bent down and gently lifted the sick, old, English bulldog. Peachy did not growl or struggle. "This old girl has never behaved so well." Father carefully carried his burden towards the doorway. He turned to pass through the narrow opening; halfway, he and Peachy paused. "I think I'm stuck." Father twisted this way and that. Each movement wedged man and dog tighter.

"Back up and let me try," I said.

Father complied, but his coat snagged on a sharp piece of board. We heard a loud rip; Father and Peachy blocked the only exit out of this dank, frigid mausoleum, and Mrs. Pewter and I stood frozen and trapped. From somewhere behind us came a rustle of leaves and a shrill squeak, then scuttling sounds. Mrs. Pewter sprang into action. She grabbed Peachy from Father's arms and thrust the shivering animal at me. I clutched the dog as Mrs. Pewter ran toward Father like a battering ram. She rushed at Father and stripped off his coat in a blur of rapid motion. One hard shove and Father was outside with the housekeeper a hairsbreadth behind. Then Mrs. Pewter's strong arms reached through the gap in the mausoleum doorway and grabbed Peachy. The housekeeper sprinted out of the graveyard carrying the thirty-five-pound English bulldog, and they traversed the three blocks to the Vicarage in record time. She never looked back.

Father and I watched with our mouths agape. "Should we hurry after her, do you suppose?"

"I don't think that's necessary. We can take a few minutes to search in the mausoleum, surely," Father said. "But here, Alberta, take my overcoat. You'll catch your death." Father slung the black broadcloth over my shoulders. I appreciated the comforting warmth as it hung over my frozen red fingers. "Alberta, look here," Father said from across the room, "a greasy sack filled with a bit of meat. Someone was obviously feeding Peachy."

I squatted down and picked up a small paper wrapper. I inspected it closely. "It's a small envelope, the kind you get from the Chemist's." I pinched it open and shone the light on the paper. "Traces of white powder. Peachy wasn't sick from exposure; someone drugged her."

"Who would go to all that trouble?"

"According to Mrs. Crumpet, Martin Goolsby."

"Martin wouldn't do a thing like this. I know you don't care for him, but he's harmless."

"He gives me the willies."

"That's because he has a yen for you."

"Oh, pooh, that's ridiculous."

"No, I think you're unfair to Martin."

"Hmm," I said as I resumed my search of the mausoleum floor.

I panned my light this way and that, kicking aside clumps of rotted leaves. Father and I searched in silence for a few minutes.

"We'll that like looks the lot," Father said, as he stood and rubbed the small of his back, "and I'm getting chilled to the bone. Let's get home and see how Peachy and Mrs. Pewter are getting on."

"Wait, just a second, Father. I saw something right over by the door. Aw, here we are." I scooted leaves aside with the metal ferrule of my umbrella. Father leaned down and picked up the round white object. "A marble?" I asked.

Father rubbed the object on his pant leg to remove a coating of slime and leaf fragments. "Here, Alberta, shine your light on it now. It's a pearl. What in the world would a pearl be doing in the Grimwood Mausoleum?"

The Return of Peachy

Father and I drove up Pickering Street in Bert's taxi. As we drew close to Number 14, tears welled up in my eyes, and a knot formed in my throat. The wicker laundry basket at my feet rustled and creaked as Peachy lifted her head and squirmed a bit. "Almost home, Peachy, honey. I think she knows," I said to Father.

The black Model T pulled up to the curb. Father leaned forward and handed the taxi driver eight pence. "Here you go, Bert, thanks."

"Oh, anytime, Vicar Holdaway. Glad to help Mrs. Crumpet. She sets a lot of store by that silly dog."

Father slid out of the cab and came around to open my door. I clambered out, and then we reached into the automobile, and each grabbed a basket handle. "Ugh, this dog weighs a ton. I don't know how Mrs. Pewter managed all by herself."

"Terror," I said as Father and I lugged the basket up the cement steps. Father did a polite staccato on the mahogany front door.

"Coming, coming," a shaky voice called. The front door

opened slowly. Mrs. Crumpet looked at the basket suspended between Father and me. She saw Peachy's bulging, bloodshot eyes, the grin on her face, and the fang that peaked at the corner of her slobbery mouth. The dog's stubby tail wagged. "Oh, Peachy," Mrs. Crumpet stepped back into the hall, sat on a hideous Victorian chair, and pulled a hankie out of her apron pocket. She held the hankie to her eyes and wept.

Father and I stepped inside, closed the door, and set the creaky basket on the floor. I knelt by Mrs. Crumpet and put my arm around her shaking shoulders. "Now, now, please don't do that; Peachy's fine, really."

The old woman took a shuddering breath and dabbed at her eyes. "Oh, my, excuse me for being so silly. I knew you and the Vicar would find Peachy, but so soon."

Peachy heard her name and struggled out of the basket. Father hefted the large, white English bulldog out of her makeshift bed. The dog took a few steps forward and swayed, gazing at her owner. Then Peachy shook herself and piddled on the floor. "Oh, Peachy, darling," the elderly woman knelt beside her bemused pet.

"Here, Mrs. Crumpet, let me carry her somewhere," Father said.

"Peachy's bed is back in the kitchen by the stove."

"Sounds a good spot. She is still a bit rummy, I'm afraid." Father lifted the dog, carried her through the swinging kitchen door, and then laid her gently in the quilt-lined box. "There you are, Peachy, ma' girl."

"Why would she be rummy?" Mrs. Crumpet said as she and I followed Father into the kitchen.

"We found her near the Vicarage. It seems someone fed Peachy some meat laced with a pinch of sleeping draught. She

25

was pretty groggy when we found her, but she's perking up."

"Martin Goolsby?"

"We really have no idea."

"He works part-time at the Chemist's," said Mrs. Crumpet.

"But that doesn't necessarily follow," said Father. "Most people have a sleeping powder in their medicine chest. Why would Martin want to do such a thing?"

"Martin hates Peachy."

I looked at Father and gave a slight shake of my head. "We'll ask around. Maybe someone saw something. But it's best to say nothing until we know for sure, don't you agree?"

"I suppose so," Mrs. Crumpet said with reluctance. "Just so I have my Peachy back."

"Yip," said Peachy from deep within her quilt. We all laughed, and the bulldog thumped her tail. Then she looked up at Father and gave a low, throaty growl.

"Whoa-ho," Father chuckled, "I guess Peachy's getting back to her old self."

"Yes, I'd say that's a good sign."

The three of us sauntered to the front door. "I am more than grateful to you both. If there is anything I can ever do."

"Just keep Peachy under control and keep your windows covered," I said with a smile.

"I will do, my dear," Mrs. Crumpet said as she reached up to envelop me in a warm hug. "And I'll see you in church, Vicar Holdaway."

Father jerked to a halt, a look of indecision on his face. "Well, I-I may as well tell you, I'll be leaving in a few weeks."

"Leaving on vacation? Oh, I am so glad. We have, the congregation has, I should say, been so concerned for you these past few months. I'm glad you'll be getting a little respite from all of our problems."

"Thank you so much; I appreciate that. Vicar Featherstone will replace me. He's a fine fellow; you'll like him."

We heard a bark from the kitchen as Mrs. Crumpet opened the front door and followed Father and me onto the porch. "Thank you again, Ambrose, Alberta. Come back to us soon; I don't know how we'll make it through this awful war without you."

Father and I walked arm in arm down Pickering Street. At the corner, I looked back. The elderly parishioner was still on her porch; she blew a kiss and waved. I waved back. Then Father and I crossed the street and headed home to St. Hugh's.

Devonshire House

The following two weeks flew by in a flurry of activity. I spoke to Mrs. Brodie, my direct supervisor at British Red Cross headquarters, and requested a compassionate leave to help Father relocate and settle in Cornwall.

"We'll miss you, Alberta; hurry back," said Mrs. Brodie. "If you must stay in Cornwall for an extended period, let me know. We can put you to work locally, raising money, maybe. You know how chronically short of funds we are. In fact, now that I think about it, several of our fundraising personnel are in London to meet and discuss the newest plan." Mrs. Brodie's eyes widened in excitement, and a faint blush touched her cheeks. "We will put out an appeal to the public for pearls. We plan to make a necklace to be auctioned to raise money for the sick and wounded. I believe one of the girls, a.... let me see," Mrs. Brodie flipped through some papers on her desk, "a Miss Flora Hicks, is here from Cornwall. I will see if a meeting can be arranged."

"That would be fine, Mam; anything I can do to help."

"Binky Penrose has family in Lanmorech, doesn't she?" asked Mrs. Brodie. "Hmm, yes, Lord and Lady Penrose have been most supportive and helpful to our Voluntary Aid Detachment in the area. You'd do well to get in touch with them. Now, if you'll excuse me, Alberta," Mrs. Brodie sighed and gave me a rueful smile, "I have another meeting."

"Oh, yes, of course, thank you." I smiled as I stood and held out my hand.

Mrs. Brodie took it between her own and gave me a reassuring pat. "Give my love to your father."

I left Mrs. Brodie's office in the former library of the palatial home of the Duke of Devonshire. The Duke had donated the main floor of Devonshire House to the British Red Cross for its headquarters. Down the hall and to the right was the Grand Ballroom, but dancing stayed far from anyone's thoughts. Walls bare and chandeliers draped in muslin, the large echoing room, once a center of frivolity, was all business. Row upon row of wooden worktables, which held row upon row of bulging file boxes, filled the prestigious gilt room. At the farthest corner sat my desk and squeaky oak office chair. I flicked on my desk lamp, sat down, then leaned back and rubbed my temples, unsure how much to delegate and clear away.

"You're leaving?" said a familiar voice from behind me. I twirled halfway in my chair and nodded to my good chum, Lady Lawanda "Binky" Penrose. She placed a hand on my shoulder; there was a look of concern on her face. "What's going on?"

"Father is taking a sabbatical to Cornwall. To Lanmorech, as a matter of fact."

"Lanmorech, why in the world would the Vicar of St. Hugh's go to Lanmorech?"

"Let me clear my desk, then we can go to lunch, and I'll fill you in on all the details."

"Right, there are a few things I need to finish and return to Mrs. Brodie. Give me half an hour." Binky rushed off to her workstation and started clacking away on her typewriting machine.

A while later, my correspondence completed and readied for the post; I covered the typewriter, closed up my tidied desk, and switched off my light. Binky remained hunched over her machine, pencil behind her ear, deep in concentration. I waited until the carriage return went 'ding' and Binky waved the piece of foolscap. "Done," she said.

We both gathered our coats and rushed out into the afternoon bustle of Piccadilly. We headed straight for Brewster's tea house. Brewster's was 'the' place for working gentlewomen to eat, have tea and socialize. There was always a queue at lunchtime, but even with wartime shortages, you could expect something delectable on the menu. Binky and I stood just inside the double doors and waited in line for a table. There was a sibilant hiss of female chatter, the clink of silver cutlery, and the scent of hearty vegetable soup, which was today's special. My stomach growled. Binky poked me in the ribs with her elbow, "Over there," she said, "a table." Before I could stop her, she threw a napkin over the reserved sign in the middle of the snowy white tablecloth.

My cheeks burned as the attendant came over to take our order. Binky behaved just as usual and ordered today's "special" for us both. The waitress didn't bat an eye; she just took the reserved sign, napkin, and all and slipped it into her apron pocket.

"Now," Binky said, eyebrows raised, "tell-all."

"Well, Father and I are going down to Lanmorech to reopen Highdrift. He has been feeling unwell, and the Bishop has granted him a leave to recuperate."

"So, how long will you stay?" Binky asked as she shook out her napkin and laid it on her lap.

"Not more than a few weeks, we'll see. It depends on how much work there is to do on the house and if we can find someone to housekeep for Father."

"Oh, just ask Granny. She knows everyone and tells everyone what they should do; nicely, of course. She has an imperious way about her. No one brooks her displeasure. She's a marvelous museum piece."

The waitress brought two enormous bowls filled with piping hot soup. Then she set a small basket with a couple of rolls in the center of the table. Binky and I eyed them with suspicion. White flour was discouraged, and these rolls had a dark and heavy appearance. "What's in them, do you suppose?"

"Must be the barley flour; just crumble them up in your soup, and it won't matter." I plucked one out of the basket, held the roll to my nose, and sniffed, "Smells good and doesn't feel too heavy." I took a pinch and popped the yeasty-scented morsel into my mouth. "Mmm, not bad, a bit bland but will be great in the soup." I crumbled the remaining roll into my bowl and tasted it. "Soup's good too."

Binky poked around in her bowl, "No meat, just lentils. Scuttlebutt has it that a Ministry of Food Control will be established soon. Which means this war may continue for a long time."

"Makes our problems pretty insignificant."

"Yes, it does," Binky nodded.

"I guess we do all we can wherever we find ourselves. If I end up in Lanmorech overlong, Mrs. Brodie encouraged me to help with Red Cross fundraising."

"Good idea; when are you leaving?" Binky asked between mouthfuls.

"Shortly, on Thursday, late. We are taking the *Night Riviera*."

"Oh, lovely, that's my favorite trip. Have you ever been?"

"No, not to Cornwall or on the sleeper train."

"Father, Olivia, and Granny may also be on that train. They are moving to Penrose House for the duration." Binky continued, "You be sure Vicar Holdaway checks to see if Father is on the train. They haven't visited in ages, and Granny dotes on the vicar. They can have a good 'gas,' which should perk your father up to no end. Granny will have tons of things to keep him busy while he's in Lanmorech. You'll see." Binky finished her soup and raised her hand to signal our waitress, "Coffee, please, for two." Then she reached over and patted my hand. "Now you have a nice trip to Cornwall, and don't worry about a thing."

Paddington Station

⁓⦿⦿⦿⁓

Even at this late hour, Paddington Station echoed with excitement. The iconic round leaded glass station clock showed 11:40, twenty minutes before departure. I slowed my pace to scan the milling crowd and leaned on the wrought-iron railing at the head of the stairs to Platform 1. There were scads of khaki-clad servicemen and even a few women and children, but I did not see Father. I set my suitcase on the pavement, smoothed my hair, straightened my brown felt hat, and resumed my progress. Out of nowhere came a brutal shove. *Wham*, my body slammed into the iron stair rail. I sank in a heap to the ground and lay there dazed. Time and space slowed, voices and depot noises slurred like a gramophone record played at half speed. My mind focused on the vast glass and iron arches forming the cathedral-like ceiling. The Art Nouveau tracery and sun and moon cutouts soared high above, and from somewhere far away, a loudspeaker called, "*Night Riviera,* leaving Platform 1, all aboard for Penzance."

33

Strangers crowded around, and one woman in uniform bent over me, "Here, let's give Miss Holdaway some room." She waved the onlookers aside. "Now, miss, let's just sit up slowly and see how we feel."

I closed my eyes to stop the swirling; and tried to say something but couldn't catch my breath. An arm slipped under my shoulders to guide me. I leaned against the iron stair rail for a few moments as my benefactress chafed my hands. "You poor thing, are you all right? Your hands are like ice."

"I'm all right, just a little dizzy." I touched the large, tender knot on my forehead. My fingers encountered something wet and sticky. My eyes flew open, blood. I don't do well with blood, especially my own.

"Last call for Penzance," came the crackly voice over the loudspeaker.

I struggled to stand. "That's my train. My father is on that train. He's expecting me."

"Oh, but …," said the woman shaking her head, "you are so pale, and your forehead, you're bleeding."

I rose to my knees, then to my feet. I swayed as I grabbed the woman's arm with one hand and searched my coat pocket with the other.

"Here," the woman said, "I have a handkerchief." She dabbed at the graze. "It doesn't look too bad, but I don't know …?"

"I'm much better; it was the surprise more than anything." I smiled at the woman as I picked up my suitcase. "Thank you for your help, but I simply must catch that train to Penzance."

"Well, if you're sure," the woman took hold of my elbow, "but I am personally going to put you on that train and get someone to keep an eye on you. And hand over that luggage," she said with a smile.

I did as she requested. We shuffled down the stairs, out onto the concourse, and along to Platform 1, where the *Night Riviera* was about to depart. The woman left me and hurried past the steaming and puffing engine. She walked to the end of the train car and stopped to speak to someone silhouetted in the doorway. Then she beckoned me forward. I reached my compartment and shook the woman's hand. "Thank you so much." I had no time to say more. The train attendant took my case, guided me on board, and shut and latched the outer door. I sank gratefully onto the tapestry-covered bench seat. I closed my eyes and leaned back, sitting quietly and still, trying not to cry. The train shook with the motions of departure. Next came the creaks and sway of acceleration and the mesmerizing cradle-like rocking.

After a while, the sound of a rolling cart and clanking china warned me I was no longer alone. I opened my eyes and saw the kindly porter, "Here we go, Miss, a nice cup of tea and a headache powder." The porter crossed the compact cabin and flipped up a little wooden tabletop that lay flat under the picture window. He deftly slid the tea tray onto the gleaming surface. "And I brought you something else, too," the little man said as he stepped aside.

"Hello, my dear," said Father, his face full of concern. "What has happened to you? Dodd here tells me you had an accident."

"Thank goodness you're here, Father! I feel so strange. Someone pushed me from behind. I stopped at the top of the stairs to check the time, and someone pushed me from behind. I wanted to ask the nice woman that helped me if she saw anything, but I didn't get the chance."

"Whoa now, Alberta, slow down; you're not making much sense." Father turned to speak to the porter. "Thanks, Dodd, for all your help," he said as he slid him a nice tip.

"Here, Sir, let me make up the upper berth for you real quick-like." The porter unlocked the upper, smoothed the bedding, fluffed the pillow, and turned on the tiny reading light at the head of the bunk. "There we go then. Make sure to ring if you need help with anything, Sir, Miss." The porter bowed and left the compartment.

"We will. Thanks again," I said with a strained smile. As soon as the porter shut the door, my vision blurred, and I fell back on the blue-patterned banquette. The rocking of the train and its incessant rhythmic clacking over the tracks made it difficult for me to maintain consciousness; I slid sideways.

"Alberta, Alberta dear," Father knelt and touched my face.

"I'm fine, Father; I just need some rest." Father removed my shoes and coat. He gently raised my head, slid a pillow against the armrest, and then covered me with a blanket. A light tinkle of water came from the tiny corner sink. A moment later, there was a gentle dabbing at the graze on my forehead. Then blessed darkness. Father had switched off the overhead cabin light. I fell asleep.

My eyes snapped open. The luminous dial of my lapel watch said 2:23. The inside of the cabin was dark as a London blackout except for a thin line of light under the compartment door. I lay in my half-made berth and let my eyes adjust. I touched tentative fingers to the tender knot on my forehead, then eased myself upright, slid back the blanket, and waited, hunched over, head bowed. The motion of the train rocked me, but the dizziness had subsided. My stomach contracted in a spasm of hunger. I stood and placed a light hand on the upper berth for support, shuffled the few steps to the compartment door, opened it, and stuck my head out. Should I ring for an attendant? The hallway was empty. What does one do on a train at 2 a.m. when one needs to go to the "ladies" and would kill for a cup of tea?

I couldn't bring myself to disturb anyone. I stepped back into the dark coziness of the compartment and listened. The cabin was as quiet as Grimwood mausoleum. I held my arms out and took the few steps from the door to the banquette, then lightly touched the upper berth. I sighed and laid my head on my outstretched arm. Father's berth was empty.

"Well," I said, "I'll just have to find him." I flicked on the table lamp. A triangle of light shone on the tips of my shoes, which peeked from under the edge of my berth. I slipped them on and glanced in the mirror above the sink. My hair stuck out like a madwoman's. I yanked the pins from my loose chignon, tamed the wavy mess with my fingers into one long plait, and arranged my bangs to cover my bruised forehead. I grabbed my jacket from where it hung on the coat hook by the window, then checked again in the mirror, smoothing myself down as best I could, and headed out the door.

The train's corridor stretched to the right. I swayed down the hallway, grabbing hold of the smooth wooden handrail that ran underneath the windows. In the middle of the forty-foot sleeper car was a ladies' Salle de Bain. I paid a quick visit. On the wall in the small lounge was a detailed diagram of the train; it showed the restaurant's location. I'd search there for Father and get a cup of tea for myself.

I continued my wobbly progress down the hallway, then stepped into a small vestibule. The noise and the racketing motion of the train intensified. For the first time, I felt the fierce power of the steam locomotive, the elemental sensation of barreling down two steel rails at sixty miles an hour. The silence seemed extreme when I lifted the handle and stepped into the comparative quiet of the next sleeper car. I sashayed with increasing skill down another long corridor, passed through another vestibule, and finally entered the Dining Car.

Plush blue velvet curtains framed each picture window, and a rectangular table for four flanked by luxurious high-backed chairs sat underneath. The white tablecloth, starched and creased, light blue china emblazoned with GWR, gleaming silver cutlery, and white linen napkins completed the tableau. All that was missing were the passengers; the Dining Car was empty. As I approached the doorway at the other end, which led (so the tasteful sign above the archway informed me) to the Lounge Car, a voice raised in alarm made me pause.

"I don't know what you mean!" the unseen woman protested. "I would never tell him that. Those pearls…" A low, unintelligible voice cut the comment off like the flip of a switch. I felt a rush of air as the door ahead opened and closed. Embarrassed to be caught eavesdropping, I waited a minute before I continued. I entered the Lounge; it, too, was almost empty at this late hour. Only two other sleepless souls occupied the intimate group of low tables and soft chairs. Their whispered tête-à-tête halted; the eyes of the gentlemen turned towards me. I tried to appear unconcerned, but my cheeks burned as I headed straight for the only other person in the room; Dodd, the steward, now acting as bartender.

Dodd noticed me as I approached the gleaming oak counter. Behind the bar was a huge plate glass mirror that reflected the entire room, including the staring men, who dropped their heads and resumed conversation. "Miss Holdaway," Dodd greeted me like a long-lost friend, "are you feeling better?"

I smiled at the steward. "Mmm," I nodded, "so much better. May I get a cup of tea at this late hour?"

"That's about all you can get. We stop serving alcohol right after we leave Paddington. What about a snack? I'm sure we can rustle up something for you."

"I would truly appreciate that," I said. "Has my father, Vicar Holdaway, been here?"

"Oh, yes, Miss, he was chatting with that nice couple from Lanmorech. They take this train frequently, especially Lord Penrose; he works for the War Department."

"Oh, I see."

"Excuse me, Miss, here's your tea. I'll just scoot back to the kitchen and see what I can find."

"Thank you so much, Dodd." I took a sip of my tea and then glanced in the mirror. The two gentlemen were leaving. I wondered what had happened to the couple I heard arguing.

As I sat at the bar and sipped my tea, the energy seemed to drain out of my body. Outside, inky black shadows and forms flashed past. The high scream of a train whistle cut through the night. The dizziness returned. I wished I had stayed in my cabin and rang the bell.

Dodd returned with a small tray of sandwiches. "Here you are, Miss; these food shortages are taking their toll, but we can always find something in the kitchen for a late-night snack."

"Mmm, thank you, looks wonderful. I heard rumblings at Red Cross headquarters about the possibility of food rationing."

Dodd shook his head. "There's talk of shutting down the train service too. That would be a shame for a lot of reasons."

I nodded as I nibbled at the corner of a small tea sandwich, "Dodd?"

"Yes, Miss?"

"As I was coming into the Dining Car, I heard two people in a heated argument. The woman sounded upset. I wondered if you noticed anything shortly before I came in."

"I didn't see anyone but the two gentlemen at the table at the back. I'm not here the whole time, though. I spend a lot of time in the kitchen area and might have missed them."

"Where could they have gone?"

"That's a good question. Beyond here, there's only the kitchen, the Postal car, and the Observation car, no sleepers."

I finished my sandwich and cup of tea and said good night to Dodd. Once more, I swayed down the aisles through connecting passages and finally down the narrow hallway of dark windows, gleaming paneling, and brass doorknobs to compartment number 27.

The small table light was on. Father sat bolt upright in the upper berth, a look of concern on his face.

"Alberta, where, in the name of all that's holy, have you been? I was about to pull the emergency cord!"

"I was looking for you." I sank onto my bunk, slipped off my shoes, and lay down, too tired to scold Father, too tired even to change my clothes.

"Are you all right? I was talking to Bertram Penrose two doors down in number 29, came back to check on you, and you were gone."

"I'm fine, just sleepy."

Father's voice droned on, but I lost track of what he said.

"Alberta?" A warm hand brushed my forehead. I opened my eyes, surprised to see daylight. Father's spaniel eyes stared into mine. "Good morning." I moaned and turned my back to him. "Breakfast will be here any minute." There was a discrete rap on the door. Quickly, I pulled the sheet over my head. "Come in," Father called.

"Good mornin' sir, nice day ain't it." A cart rattled into the room. I slid the sheet down to my nose as the waitress nodded. "Nice hot coffee, Miss. No sugar, though, I'm afraid." She deftly set Father's breakfast on the table. "Now, Mr. Dodd says you're feelin' a bit 'iffy,' so's I brought you a tray."

I struggled to sit. "Oh, how nice."

"Coo, we do look a bit peaky, and your eye, you poor thing!" She laid the tray on my lap, then turned and gave Father a dirty look. The waitress wheeled the trolley back out into the corridor and shut the door with a snap.

I laughed.

"Oh my, who knows what tales will fly about that eye."

"Does it look so bad?"

"Turn here; let me see in the light." I turned towards Father and lifted my face. "The eye's not that bad, but the knot on your forehead is worse."

"Oh dear, at least I don't know anyone in Lanmorech. We can go to the Inn and relax, maybe take a stroll over to Highdrift. I can't wait to see the house."

"Well…," Father peered at me over the top of his glasses, "I spoke to the Penroses last night and accepted an invitation."

"Not for today?"

Father nodded. "Yes, but you needn't go. Beatrice Penrose, Dowager Lady Penrose, I should say, requested that I make an appearance and say a few words. It's a church function to raise money for your British Red Cross. She said something about a sale and some pearl display or other."

"Pearls?" I tensed; my heart skipped a beat. "Oh, 'those' pearls," I relaxed, "The ones for the Red Cross fund. Funny how you see something once, like that pearl in Grimwood Mausoleum when we found Peachy, and then the same sort of thing crops up time and again."

"What crops up time and again?" Father asked between bites of toast.

"Pearls," I said.

Lanmorech

Father and I disembarked at Penzance. We had Father's trunks sent on to Highdrift and stood waiting outside the train station, our suitcases in a jumble at our feet.

"Mmm, someone should be here to meet us." Just as the words left Father's mouth, footsteps approached.

"Ambrose!"

"Kenwyn, you old dog!" Father and the stocky middle-aged man in country tweeds did some hearty backslapping. "Kenwyn Ott, my daughter, Alberta." Father drew me forward. "Kenwyn is the proprietor of the Moorstone Inn and a very old friend of your mother's and mine."

Mr. Ott took my hand in his rough and callused one, "You've a look of your mother," he said as his eyes searched my face. "The same sweet smile. You've not her hair, though. My, you could see that glowing red hair from a fair distance. And I don't remember your ma havin' a lump on the noggin either."

Instinctively my hand touched the bump, and my cheeks grew warm. I opened my mouth in surprise and then laughed, "No, the bumps all my own."

Mr. Ott put his arm around my shoulder and hugged me. He noticed my sharp intake of breath and my wince of pain.

"Alberta had a run-in with the stair rail at Paddington Station. She's a bit stiff and sore today," Father said.

"Ah, my Maudie will fix her up. We have a bathtub at the Moorstone as big as a swimmin' pool. That's what you need, a nice long soak." With that, Mr. Ott picked up our cases, two under each arm, and loped to his wagon. Our route took us along the picturesque Cornish coast. We entered the small town of Lanmorech and pulled into the courtyard of the Moorstone Inn. Maud, Kenwyn's wife, greeted us warmly and then showed us to our suite of rooms. As promised, Mrs. Ott hustled me off to the tub "big as a swimmin' pool." She filled it with hot water and sprinkled in some epsom salts for good measure. After a nice long soak, she fed me and bundled me off to bed.

My sleep was hard and dreamless. My eyes opened with a snap. Where was I? My hand rubbed over the sheet, stiff from the clothesline. It released the fragrance of fresh sea air and springtime. That's right; I was in Lanmorech at the Moorstone. I pushed off the covers, slid off the high bedstead, and stood on the chilly stone floor. My bare feet crossed the cobbles to the sitting room; Father was not there. I tapped on his bedroom door; there was no answer. Back in my room, I checked the time. It was past one o'clock; I'd slept more than three hours. Father must be at the church sale by now. As I dressed, the stiffness eased, and my head cleared. I'd take a walk to the church and find Father.

St. Tancred's dated from medieval times. Built of the same moorstone as the inn, it stood solid and forbidding at the end of town. All signs for the "Sale of All Work" pointed to the quaint and practical auditorium next door.

Sunshine streamed through the mullioned windows of the old parish hall. It brightened the already snowy white cloths on tables aligned in military precision around half-timbered walls. A bevy of shoppers buzzed about tables in the center of the room piled high with jumble sale items. I scanned the crowd for Father's slim, black-clad figure. He stood conspicuously alone in the far corner by the exit door. I waved a quick wave and headed toward him. A noisy queue of young girls waiting in the tea line blocked my progress.

"Excuse me, might I get through?" I asked with a smile. The girls ignored me and continued talking to the plump, frowzy woman presiding over the tea booth.

"Oh, Mrs. Jollie," said the tallest and prettiest of the girls, "you look so nice today, love your hair. How do you get that delightful frizz in front?" Behind her, the other girls snickered quietly and poked one another.

"Do you really like it, miss? Had it done special up ta' Penzance. Can give you the name of the gal that I went to if ya' like," replied the older woman, eyes wide and cheeks turning pink.

My cheeks started to burn; my heart thumped in my chest. "Excuse me," I said in my most refined drawl as I elbowed my way to the front of the tea line. I extended my hand to Mrs. Jollie, "Hello, so lovely to meet you, Mrs. Jollie. I'm Vicar Holdaway's daughter, Alberta."

"Nice to meet you, Miss Holdaway, I'm sure," replied Mrs. Jollie. "May I get you a cup of tea then, all proceeds for the Red Cross?"

"Yes, please, I would like to compliment you, Mrs. Jollie, on your lovely table and all you're doing for the Red Cross. Mrs.

45

Brodie said to me just the other day that raising funds for the Red Cross would be of the utmost importance for our future success in this war. And you, young ladies," I asked, turning to speak to the young women behind me, "what have you done for the war effort besides consuming Mrs. Jollie's delightful tea?"

All six girls, including the tallest and prettiest, stood open-mouthed at my challenge. Then one of them said, "We haven't even done that much since someone rudely cut in line."

Mrs. Jollie gasped, "Well, I never; you girls can be rude to me but to insult a newcomer and the Vicar's daughter, get away with you!" she said, shooing the girls away with her hands.

The girls turned and crossed the room in a huddle, whispering and giggling behind their hands. "I seem to be driving your customers away, Mrs. Jollie," I said, "but here comes my Father to meet you; hopefully, he will purchase something."

"Hello, my dear."

"Ah, Father, I'd like you to meet Mrs. Jollie. We must both buy some of these luscious goodies because I'm afraid I just drove away a whole gaggle of young customers whose healthy appetites are going elsewhere for their tea."

"Oh ho, up to your old tricks again, are you ma' dear keeping all the sweeties for yourself," said Father, smiling as he put his arm around my shoulders. "I'd love some tea, and so nice to meet you, Mrs. Jollie."

Mrs. Jollie's face turned pink again as she beheld the tall and distinguished vicar. "So nice to meet you, I'm sure, sir, and the tea's my treat. Your lovely daughter came to my rescue like an avenging angel; she did. Saving me from the taunts and teases of our local gentry, home on their holidays and bored, looking for someone to pick on. Young women didn't behave that way when I was a girl. The world's a changeable place," said Mrs.

Jollie shaking her head as she handed the vicar his steaming cup. "I hear you're doing up Highdrift."

Father choked on his tea, "How did you...?"

"I work at the manor, and Mrs. Ott, the housekeeper, always gets the news first. When I heard someone was reopening Highdrift, it gave me the shivers. You wouldn't catch me there after dark."

Just then, there was a commotion at the entrance door. The crowd parted like water sliced by the prow of a battleship. Indeed, the grand dame, built along imposing lines, caused quite a stir. The aristocratic juggernaut crossed the parish hall and walked up the short flight of stairs to the stage. "Welcome, welcome one and all," said the booming voice. "I am Lady Beatrice Penrose, and on behalf of the Lanmorech Parish Council and the British Red Cross, and St. John's Ambulance, I would like to encourage you to spend freely and eat heartily; the exact opposite of what you've been required to do since the war started." The crowd politely laughed, cheered, and clapped. Lady Penrose raised her hands, and the crowd quieted, "Also, there will be an auction in an hour or so, and we will be treated to a display of the Red Cross pearl necklace collection that Miss Flora Hicks has curated. As you all know, Flora has worked tirelessly to organize this event and other Red Cross fundraisers. Let us give her a big hand." The crowd erupted again with murmurs and clapping, "Flora, Flora Hicks," called Lady Penrose. "Ah well, she must be fluttering around organizing or something. We will have her give her little talk later. For now, keep shopping and remember, 'Put the Pay in Patriotism.'" Lady Penrose gave a final flutter of her hands and left the stage amid more applause.

"Where is that stupid girl," snarled Lady Penrose, *sotto voice,* to her secretary Miss Briggs. Miss Briggs scuttled behind her employer and barely had a chance to stutter a few "uh's" and "oh's" before her ladyship was off again. "To miss her own presentation; Well, that is the last time I will let the Council persuade me to give an outsider complete control. See what it's gotten us, Briggs?"

Lady Beatrice Flips Her Lid

I finished my tea and fairing biscuit and got up from the table where Father sat, cornered by Mr. Alfred Ott, the mayor of Lanmorech. Highdrift was almost devoid of furnishings, so I slowly strolled up and down the aisles of the jumble sale. In amongst lamps without shades, chipped teacups, and lidless teapots, I found a few treasures. An embroidered tablecloth edged in tatting, a practical-looking brass oil lamp that swiveled, and a bright patchwork quilt. After every purchase, I trotted over to Father and deposited my finds on the table in front of him.

"Mmm, nice lamp; for my desk, I hope," he said.

"Yes, of course," I said, smiling. "Is there a desk at Highdrift?"

"Not yet," said Father with eyebrows raised in challenge.

"There is a nice desk in the back of the Parish Hall with the auction items," said Mr. Ott, "also bookcases, trunks, and a whole dining set with a buffet from up at the Manor."

"That sounds a bit grand for Highdrift, but I adore looking."

Mr. Ott yelled across the room, "Ey, Saben, come here, man." I lifted my gaze. A man across the room turned and held up his hand in greeting. He was tall, about thirty, and very slim, with close-cropped, dark hair. He loped over towards Mr. Ott, greeting people as he went. As he neared the table, I saw the red puckered scar that ran from his lower jaw to his ear.

"Ey, here's our war hero," said Mr. Ott. "Saben Best, this is Vicar Holdaway and his daughter Alberta, just newly come to this parish."

"Nice to meet you both," said Saben holding out his hand to the Vicar and nodding to me. "And no war hero just damned lucky, excuse me, Miss," he said.

"I was wonderin' if you'd oblige by taking Miss Alberta backstage to see the furniture. Saben knows a bit about such things," Mr. Ott said, "he helped his da fixing and tinkering for years."

"Oh, I really don't need an escort," I said, shaking my head. I could feel my cheeks growing warm, "I'm quite capable…."

"I'm sure you are, Miss," Saben interrupted," but I am headed back there for a look-see, so how about if I tag along with you?"

I knew there was no way to refuse without being ungracious, so I inclined my head and smiled, "Let's go then, thank you."

Saben stepped aside and waited for me to precede him. We walked single file until we reached the outer rim of the hall. Saben looked up and saw the throng of people blocking the stairs leading to the stage.

"Looks like everyone in the whole county has shown up for the festivities," he said. "We'll head outside and go around." Just as we stepped out the door, a beautiful foreign-looking woman approached Saben and threw her arms around him. She spoke in an unintelligible patois, then took his face between her hands and kissed him on each cheek very fast. "Morvah, please," said Saben, as he gently pushed the woman away, "you'll give Miss Holdaway the wrong impression."

"Miss Holdaway?" The woman put her hand in the pocket of her long, full, striped skirt and brought out a pair of glasses; she slid them on her aquiline nose. "I thought she was Flora Hicks." I abruptly stepped back as the woman's magnified eyes looked me up and down. "You aren't Miss Hicks."

Saben Best shook his head and grinned, "That's what I said. This is Vicar Holdaway's daughter. So your performance was a total waste."

Just then, the sun faded, and a stiff breeze came up off the bay. "Brrr, the wind is cold. Let us go inside," the woman said to Saben as she took his arm and leaned against him.

"Sorry, Morvah, Miss Holdaway and I are going the other way to look at the large pieces to be auctioned."

"That's all right, Mr. Best," I said, "I'm fine on my own, really." I could see Saben stiffen at my insistence. He inclined his head, took the older woman by the arm, and led her away. The woman kept up a constant stream of chatter as the two of them walked back to the parish hall.

I sighed in relief, glad to be on my own again. I turned and went quickly up the gray stone steps, tugged at the old blackened door, and went into the back portion of the hall. The door latched, the darkness was palpable. I stood still, letting my eyes adjust, then noticed a ribbon of light. I walked towards it, reached out, and parted a pair of dusty curtains. Before me was a treasure trove of miscellany, a veritable Aladdin's cave ripe for plundering. A few others were milling about, looking under chairs, sorting through crates, flipping through stacks of paintings. Over to my right was the dining room set Mr.

Ott had mentioned. I walked over to it and ran my hand along the smooth, ice-cold marble top of the mahogany buffet. The whole set was very bulky and dark, with heavy scrollwork. Not something I could envision Father or me using at Highdrift. However, next to the mahogany was a set of wicker. Wicker was sure to be more affordable, and we could use it inside or out. There was a small couch, a chair with an ottoman, and a tall plant stand. I took note of the number 45 on the large oak tag label.

Behind the wicker was a tall armoire, beautiful but again too bulky and dark. Leaning up against the armoire was a stack of pictures. I stooped to flip through them; most were reprints of hunting scenes depicting braces of dead pheasants, hunting spaniels, and horses. The last picture was a still life, a blue and white vase full of wildflowers with a little Asian figurine in the foreground. It was bright and charming. I bent down looking for a number when a voice said, "Those will most likely be sold as a lot." I turned to see Saben Best standing behind me. I felt a sudden surge of irritation and then guilt as he kindly handed me a small tablet and pencil. "This is for jotting down lot numbers."

"Why thank you," I said." I really have no clue what I'm doing. But I do have my eye on a few things."

"If there are items you want to bid on, you need to register and get a bidding number. We take our auctions very seriously," Saben said with a smile. "Right over there, the tall lady in purple, Mrs. Ott." Saben guided me to a small rickety card table, "Mrs. Ott, this young lady and I need numbers."

Mrs. Ott looked up; she jerked her thumb toward the tall bookcase next to her. "Nice set of Dickens for you, Saben." Saben's eyebrows rose, and he forgot all about getting his number and about me. "Here, dear," said Mrs. Ott, "you fill this out, and I'll do Saben's, and you'll be all set. I'm Mrs. Ott. You must be Vicar Holdaway's daughter."

I held out my hand, "Yes," I said.

"I saw you looking at the wicker set; it's good quality, that. Most of these items are from up at Penrose. The family is very supportive of the war effort and the British Red Cross," said Mrs. Ott.

"That's wonderful," I replied. "I work for the Red Cross in London."

"Do you know Miss Hicks then?" asked Mrs. Ott.

"I haven't met her yet," I said," but I hope to. I've had a nice letter from her. We tried to get together in London, but things never seemed to work out."

Mrs. Ott turned and scanned the few persons in the room, but apparently, none of them was Miss Hicks. "Flora, Miss Hicks, is supposed to be here helping me. She has been collecting the Red Cross pearl donations and is supposed to display them at today's fete."

Just then, I felt a grip on my shoulder and a double squeeze. That had been father's signal ever since I could remember. I put my hand up to cover his and introduced him to Mrs. Ott.

"Where's my desk?" Father asked me.

"Mrs. Ott said there's a nice specimen across the room in that murky corner. Shall we take a peek?" I asked.

"Yes, let's," Father replied, with a nod and smile for Mrs. Ott.

Father and I crossed the room arm in arm. I looked over my shoulder towards the bookcase; Dickens still held Saben Best in thrall. I turned back towards Father, "What did you and Mr. Ott gab about all this long time?"

"Ott was telling me about the war work people are doing. Seemed pleased that there would be another cleric hereabouts.

Wanted to know if I could say a few words before the auction. He gave me a list of the various fundraisers that are going on in Lanmorech."

"I was afraid Mrs. Ott would ask me to do something like that. Seems the VAD from the Red Cross was supposed to speak, but she didn't show." We stopped in front of an old oak desk piled high with fabric. As I moved the pile aside, I saw a sizable piece of upholstery material and various chintzes. "These would look nice on the wicker."

"Wicker?" Father asked.

"Oh, I spotted a wicker set I'd like to bid on. Mmm, this desk is nice, not too big. What do you think?" Just as I placed my hand on the silky smooth oak top, Mr. Ott appeared.

"Vicar Holdaway, we are ready for you," he whispered. Then louder, Mr. Ott announced, "Ladies and gentlemen, we are about to start out front. I need a few helpers to move the folding doors." Father, Saben Best, and a few other gentlemen removed the dividers, and suddenly the whole world brightened; gone was Aladdin's cave. We were on the stage looking out across the crowded jumble sale. We filed down the steps on either side and took our places out in front. I clutched my bidding number and felt my heart beat faster. My throat was dry; I looked longingly at Mrs. Jollie's tea table. Lady Penrose swept up on stage and began to introduce Father. I had a suspicion Lady Penrose would tend towards loquacity, and I knew Father did, so I assured myself I had time for a cup of tea before the bidding commenced. I sidled slowly sideways, quietly excusing myself as I went and made it to the aisle discreetly. I glanced up at Father on stage. He gave me the merest wink and smile, and I could tell he wished he were with me as I headed for refreshments.

"Well dear, did you find anything good back yonder?" asked Mrs. Jollie. "Coo, just look at your gloves."

I looked down at my once pristine gloves and pulled them off, finger by finger. "I did quite a few things, actually. But I'm feeling rather nervous about bidding."

"Sometimes people just can't quit and pay way too much for things," said Mrs. Jollie as she poured my tea. "But it all goes for a good cause."

"I'm more worried that I'll scratch my nose or wave at Father and end up with a stuffed skunk or something," I said.

Mrs. Jollie let out a loud bark of laughter and quickly put a hand over her mouth.

"Now, Mrs. Jollie," said Saben coming up behind us, "haven't I warned you before about disturbing the peace?"

"Oh, go away with you, Mr. Saben," Mrs. Jollie said, pushing Saben playfully, "I never disturbed nobody in my life!"

A burst of applause drowned out Saben's reply, and Father's voice boomed over the church hall. "Thank you; you're so kind. I am going to cut this short. I know my daughter, Alberta, is chomping at the bit to buy a lovely desk for me, so I want to get this auction started." The crowd burst out laughing, and Father continued, "Mr. Ott has given me a list of all the ways this community is giving. Lanmorech Church Funds are raised by donation and jumble sales like this one, the local Farmer's Fund, Livestock Auctions, and anything to bring in a bit of change for our soldiers through donations to the Red Cross. Concerts, magic lantern shows, vegetable marrow seed guessing contests, and now pearls, yes, pearls. Pearls donated from all across Great Britain. The goal is to join them all into one necklace to be auctioned off by Christie's, the great auction house in London."

The crowd roared and cheered at this pronouncement until Father lifted his hands to quieten them. "I agree, Bravo. Soon, we are to be treated to a display of some of these pearls by Miss Flora Hicks of the Red Cross Voluntary Aid Detachment, whom I believe you all know," the crowd murmured in agreement. "But first," Father continued, "the auction, with Mr. Alfred Ott doing the honors, shall commence."

"As a last word," Father said, "let me leave you with a quote. My daughter, Alberta, works at the British Red Cross headquarters in London at Devonshire House. When she became a VAD, she was given a copy of these words by Rudyard Kipling, which encapsulates the philosophy of the Red Cross, for whom we hold this auction." Father paused, and then his voice rang out strong and clear:

"And only the Master shall praise us.
    And only the Master shall blame.
    And no one will work for the money.
    No one will work for the fame.
    But each for the joy of the working,
    And each, in his separate star,
    Will draw the thing as he sees it.
    For the God of things as they are!"

Father gestured to Mr. Ott amidst thunderous applause. The mayor stepped forward, eyes shining with a suspicion of tears. He cleared his throat and thanked Father for the introduction. "Now that should loosen the wallets of you bidders out there. Remember, it's all for the boys." Ott raised his hands, and off he went. He jibbered and jabbered so fast that I had no idea what was happening. By the time I gulped my tea and Saben had escorted me toward the front of the hall, three items were gone. "Up next Lot #92; books." Two burly helpers drug out a small but heavy trunk.

Saben perked up beside me and got his bidding number out of the inside pocket of his jacket. "That's the Dickens," he said quietly. Again a flurry of vowels and consonants from Mr. Ott, a flick of the wrist from Saben; then I heard him mutter in a satisfied whisper, "Got 'em."

"Next up, another trunk," Mr. Ott said, "wicker, very large, and very heavy, judging by the veins popping out of Fred's neck and the groans coming from Bob." The crowd chuckled as the men drug the trunk forward. This is lot number...." Mr. Ott looked the trunk over for a number. "Hmm, no lot number." He looked around for Lady Penrose. He spotted her across the room, seated at one of the reserved tables. She was leaning over, speaking earnestly to her secretary Miss Briggs, totally oblivious to her surroundings.

Mr. Ott stepped forward, "Excuse me, Lady Penrose, if I could borrow Miss Briggs for one moment." Lady Penrose, startled, frowned at her secretary and motioned with her head for her to go forward. Miss Briggs stood up, cheeks aflame, embarrassment in every line of her body. She crossed the room and went up on stage. Mr. Ott spoke to the secretary. He gestured and pointed. Miss Briggs looked intently at the large wicker basket, shook her head, then nodded and returned to her table. The crowd was getting restless. Mr. Ott raised his hands, "Just a few moments, ladies and gentlemen, we'll get a lot number for this item and continue."

I could hear Lady Penrose giving poor Briggs a hard time as the secretary looked through her notebook. "Give me that, you stupid girl," she hissed. Lady Penrose grabbed the notebook and rushed on stage. "Here we are," she said in her high falsetto, pushing Mr. Ott aside and speaking directly to the crowd. "Now, every item was checked as it came in, and every item has a number. Ergo," she paused to let her words sink in, "this wicker trunk MUST have its number," she trilled. Dowager Lady Penrose then twirled around; she spotted Miss Briggs standing next to the offending merchandise. The lady snapped her fingers at the secretary, pointed, and then made an opening motion with her hands. Following this pantomime, Miss Briggs bent over the trunk and lifted the lid. Lady Penrose immediately rushed forward and pushed Miss Briggs aside. The Lady stuck her head in the enormous basket to find the lost number.

The next sound I heard was a bone-chilling scream. Lady Penrose spun around like a leaf blown in the wind and screamed again and again and again. Her face turned ruddy red and then ghostly white.

Saben jumped up and ran forward toward the stage. As he ran, he grabbed a tablecloth from a reserved table, sending items crashing and flying across the floor. Saben leaped onto the stage and threw the cloth over the open trunk. The fabric twirled in the air and then shrouded the wicker coffin and the pathetic dead woman that lay briefly exposed within it.

Miss Briggs stepped towards her hysterical employer. She grabbed Lady Penrose by both arms, spun her around, and shook her. Lady Penrose's screams turned to ragged, dragging sobs. I could hear people around me start to yell and move forward. Saben raised his hand to speak when a thunderous slap echoed throughout the auditorium. It is hard to say who looked more shaken at that moment; Lady Penrose, whose face bore a flaming red hand print, or Miss Briggs herself, with tears running down her own pale cheeks.

Highdrift

Father and I left the inn early that next morning for Highdrift. We walked side-by-side down the rough cobblestone street, which ran the length of Lanmorech's town square. A misty fog flowed from Morwenna Bay; the gloomy atmosphere matched our mood. Neither of us spoke. We just walked, each of us absorbed in somber thoughts. The only sounds were our even footfalls and the pounding surf some distance ahead.

Finally, Father sighed and shook his head, "Who'd have thought it?"

"Thought what?" I whispered, not wanting to break the comforting silence.

"Violence and death have become commonplace with war all about. But here in a small isolated English village. A young woman murdered; monstrous, shocking!"

"Oh, Father, let's not talk about it," I said. "I just want to get yesterday out of my mind. It was all too horrible. Poor Flora Hicks and then Lady Penrose."

"And Miss Briggs," said Father.

"Yes, and Miss Briggs. I can't imagine she'll keep her job after all that."

"No, I don't imagine she will. Maybe we can help in some way. We'll see."

We turned the corner and continued walking; shops and houses became sparse and gave way to fields of grass, gorse, and wildflowers whose scent mingled strangely with the salty brine of Morwenna Bay. The bay with its bobbing sailboats, long gray wharf, and breakwater made of huge boulders disappeared as we turned onto the side road marked by an old Rowan tree. Father and I walked a few more minutes up the dirt lane and came to a narrow break in an overgrown laurel hedge. This natural gate of waxy green leaves, covered by huge dewdrops, soaked us both, our toll for entrance.

"Should we tackle that hedge and the grass today? I need some fresh air and mindless labor," Father said. "And I'd like to clean the fireplace and maybe start a fire. I brought a mirror; I thought I'd see if I could look up the chimney. Check for nests and things. Maybe we could move in if I got the fire going and we got things dried and aired."

"I thought you wanted to wait until we were done painting and purchasing some furniture," I said.

"I'd just like to get settled and keep working on the house; it keeps my mind off things."

"I don't know; what about sleeping arrangements?" I asked. "The bed frames should be all right, but what about the mattresses? Maybe I'll go look at them." I walked up the uneven stone steps. The Victorian front door with ornate molding had an oval window covered by dirty yellowed lace. Swollen from the damp, the door had to be coaxed open. I bumped it sharply a few times with my hip; the door scraped along the floor. I stepped into the gloomy entryway and unleashed a dusty, musty odor. I lifted off the dingy lace curtain, wiped the window with it, then threw the curtain outside. I brushed the dust off my hands in satisfaction.

The hall was really quite nice, with a flagstone floor and a peaked roof with benches on either side. I stepped through an arched doorway into the main living area, crossed over to a large bank of windows, grabbed the curtains, and pulled. The rotted panels came away in my hands and sent up a cloud of choking dust. I bundled these and chucked them out the front door with the lace. Now some light could filter into the room through the mullioned windows that crossed the cottage's front. The layout was simple, one large room with a beamed ceiling, fireplace, and whitewashed walls. The floor was a dark wood dulled by dust and covered by two equally fusty carpets of an indeterminate pattern. My hands itched to roll them and chuck them out with the curtains, but there were a few pieces of furniture and heavy cases about, so I continued across the room. To my left, a stairway rose to the second-floor bedrooms; to the right, another archway led to the kitchen.

As I walked up the stairs, my hand trailed along the velvety oak railing. At the top, gloom again. The only light came from transoms over the doors of the bedrooms, one on either side of the hall. Directly on my left was a tiny closet. At the end of the hall was an unfinished storeroom. I poked my head into each of the bedrooms. The rooms were bare except for bed frames and wardrobes. The wardrobes held plenty of bedding. But there was not a mattress in sight.

I was just about to go down the hall and check the storeroom when voices floated in the open window. I saw Kenwyn Ott and Saben Best leaning against the porch, talking to Father. Mr. Ott had a rifle. "Just came by to give you a hand with the chimney," he said in a hearty tone.

"Right in here, gentlemen, let me grab this little mirror, and we'll see what we can see," Father wiped his face with his handkerchief and led the men inside. I walked down the stairs just in time to see all three men step over to the fireplace, inspect the hearth, and then the chimney flue itself. Father got on his hands and knees and put the mirror inside the chimney, checking for reflected light from above. Mr. Ott bent over and peered in as well.

Saben Best, who was staying a bit aloof from the whole process, cleared his throat. "S'cuse me, Vicar; maybe you should pull that lever there to your left."

Father reached up and pulled the lever. We all heard a loud metallic clang of a damper flipping open.

"Ey, a small bit o' light from above there, man," said Mr. Ott. "Not enough to get a good draft."

Father and Mr. Ott discussed the ramifications of the plugged chimney with Mr. Best looking on. I was superfluous, so I went outside. Father had left the clippers next to the badly overgrown Rosa rugosa and enormous honeysuckle that climbed the front of the porch. Both plants covered much of the windows. I happily snipped away and was just about to go in to see if my trimming had brightened the living room when I smelled smoke.

All three men came out on the porch arguing between bouts of coughing. "I told ya' there wasn't enough light. The chimney's blocked, man!"

"Yes, there's a blockage. Someone needs to get up on the roof and run a long brush down," said Saben.

"Sounds dangerous, and we don't have a brush," complained

Father.

"Tis dangerous and will make a mess in the house," proclaimed Mr. Ott. "Let's try the rifle. I've done it before."

"Yes, and what was the result? A hole blasted in the chimney or roof?" asked Saben.

Mr. Ott glowered, saying nothing.

"I want to clear that chimney as soon as possible; we are dead-ended until we do," said Father. All three men turned and looked at me.

I put my hands on my hips, sighed, and shook my head. "All right, help me move the table and trunks; then we can move those rugs over to the fireplace to protect the floor."

Mr. Ott had a gleeful expression on his face and rubbed his hands together in anticipation. "Right, maybe we should hang a sheet from the mantel as well."

We all turned and trooped into the cottage. We moved the heavy gate-legged table to the front of the living room windows. The trunks went to the bottom of the staircase. "I think there's a sheet in one of these," I said as I opened the lid. I rummaged around and found an old drop cloth and some books. Saben took the books and set them on the mantel as I draped the cloth across the wide fireplace opening.

Now it was Mr. Ott's turn. "Right," he said. He reached inside his jacket pocket and handed some cotton balls to Father, "For the ears." After he plugged his own, he reached for his rifle and began to load it with birdshot.

Saben looked at me, "Obviously, we aren't invited to this little party."

"I guess not. Come into the kitchen. Hopefully, we'll be out of harm's way. I'll get us some tea." As we walked down the hall, Saben stopped to look closely at one of the trunks sitting at the bottom of the stairs. He opened his mouth as if to speak but kept silent and followed me through the swinging door.

"This is a nice room," he said in surprise.

"Yes, it is. It has good bones. Lord Penrose was kind enough to send someone over to clean the kitchen and stock it with staples before we arrived, so at least I can make tea, and we can see through the windows. It's amazing how a house falls apart when it's empty."

Saben went to the sink and started working the hand pump, "Kind of like people."

"That's true," I said, unable to keep the surprise out of my voice. I held the kettle under the cold stream of spring water and then placed it on the old spirit stove to boil. "Come outside; these French doors give on to a lovely spot." We stepped out onto a flagstone terrace encircled by a low balustrade. I sat on the stone wall and felt the relaxing springtime warmth radiate through me. I rubbed my neck and lifted my face to the sun.

Saben remained standing; he put his hands in his pockets and lowered his head, "Miss Holdaway, I hate to bring this up, but I need to ask you about Flora Hicks. What did Miss Hicks do in London? Whom might she have stayed with there? Did you have acquaintances in common? That sort of thing."

I put my hand up to shade my eyes, "I never met her, so I don't know if I can help. Shouldn't the police be conducting some sort of investigation?"

"That's my job," said Saben. "I'm the local constable."

"Oh," a flush of heat spread up my neck to my face. "It's amazing how guilty that makes me feel."

Saben smiled, "It affects everyone that way at first. That's why I don't tell people."

"Unless necessary."

"Unless necessary," Saben agreed.

"Like I said," I called over my shoulder as I went inside to make our tea, "I never met her, but we both work for the Red Cross in London at Devonshire House. I do clerical work, teach first aid, and things like that. Miss Hicks does… did, fundraising. I live in London, but I think Miss Hick's moved around to various small villages. So, our paths never actually crossed. We both know Lawanda Penrose; she's a VAD and Lady Penrose's granddaughter."

"Here's a photograph of Flora Hicks," Saben handed me the picture.

We took our thick farmer's mugs of steaming tea back outside and sat down. The photo showed a plump young woman with dark hair. She stood proudly erect in her VAD uniform, squinting into the camera. A huge lump burned in my throat. I lowered my head so my hair would hide the tears forming in my eyes, then handed the photo back to Saben without looking at him. "For a minute… but no, I've never met her."

"The reason I asked is that we found a letter in the effects of Miss Hicks from Red Cross headquarters," Saben explained. "The letter informs her of your journey to Lanmorech and instructs her to meet you and your father at Paddington Station."

"Father and I weren't aware of any meeting. May I see that picture again?" Saben handed me the 2x3 inch black and white photo. I studied it closely. "I'm not sure, but it could be. I had an accident when I entered Paddington Station the night before last. A woman in a VAD uniform helped me. The woman in the photo looks similar, but I was pretty dazed. I can't be sure. Do you have any idea what happened to Flora?" I asked as I handed Saben the photograph.

"I can't discuss anything yet," Saben replied. "I'll know more tomorrow after I visit Penrose House and ask them the same questions."

"Why would Lord and Lady Penrose be involved?"

"Well, Flora Hicks was collecting those pearls for the Red Cross, and the Penroses were donating. They invited her to stay and offered to keep the collection in their safe. It just seemed to make sense." Saben said. "Those pearls are worth a lot; it would be a motive."

"Not for the Penroses, surely."

Saben opened his mouth to reply when a huge explosion came from the living room. "Oh my God." The police constable jumped up and ran into the house.

I followed close behind. Saben ran into the living room, doubled over with laughter, and pointed to the fireplace. Father and Mr. Ott had huge wads of cotton sticking out of their ears. Their faces, covered in greasy black soot, made it difficult to tell who was who. The chimney itself had a gaping hole in its front.

"You should have enough draft now," Saben said.

Father shook his head, "I give up."

I stepped around Saben and went to the fireplace to inspect the damage. The drop cloth and carpet had done pretty well at containing debris. Tiptoeing to avoid stepping on the mortar, brick shards, and soot, I gently lifted the sheet and looked up the flue. "I see light!"

"You see, man, I told you it would work," said Mr. Ott, teeth and eyes glowing in his soot-covered face. "I'll get a few bricks and fix the damage in a jiffy. Saben'll run me home, and I'll get 'er done this afternoon."

"Can I get a lift to the inn so I can get cleaned up?" asked

Father as he ineffectually wiped his face with a fine linen hankie.

"What about you?" Saben asked me.

"I think I'll stay here and get this mess cleared away. I can probably get more accomplished with you gentlemen out of here." I followed the three men to the front door. Father and Mr. Ott discussed the huge explosion with wild gestures and much laughter. Father hadn't shown so much animation for months. I smiled, shook my head, turned on my heel, went back inside, and got to work.

I took the books off the mantel and brushed traces of soot off each precious volume. The sheet fluttered down to the hearth, exposing the newly made hole and dislodging more mortar and dust. The fine particulates spiraled up and sent me into paroxysms of coughing. I went over to the bottom of the stairs and opened the largest of the trunks. I knew that I had packed linens and towels in there. Maybe I could find something to protect myself from breathing in more dust. I lifted the wicker lid, but none of its contents were familiar. The hamper was full of women's clothing. On top were a couple of white shirtwaists; a dark skirt and a jacket were next to them. I slipped my hand lightly between the clothing. As I gently moved them aside, I could see nothing to indicate to whom the trunk might belong. I was afraid to disturb things any further. Besides, I had a sinking feeling that this might have something to do with the murder of Flora Hicks.

An Unexpected Visit

I rushed around the living room to clear up the sooty mess before Father, and Mr. Ott returned to fix the chimney. I balled up the drop cloth and rolled the rugs, then dragged them down the hall, through the kitchen, and out the backdoor.

The whole time I worked, I thought about that hamper. It was like a sore tooth; I could not keep myself from probing. Yet, the more I probed, the more sensitive I became to the answers. I wished Father would get back. I stood in the middle of the kitchen with my hands cradling my elbows, trying to decide what to do next. The house creaked and groaned the way empty old houses do. A sudden gust of wind burst through the open front door and slammed the kitchen door shut. My heart lurched and pounded. Logically I knew there was nothing to fear in this place, but my unease continued to grow. I sighed and shook my head; I'd lock the house and walk back to the inn. I checked that the stove was off and went upstairs to ensure all the windows were closed. I was in what I considered my room, the room on the right with blue wallpaper when I heard women's voices in conversation. I had succeeded in scaring myself so thoroughly that my first thought was ghosts. When I looked out the window and saw two women in the backyard, I was so relieved I tapped on the window and waved ecstatically, then ran down the stairs to greet whomever they were.

To my surprise, Mrs. Jollie and Miss Briggs appeared at the kitchen door. "Well, hello," I said.

"There you are, Miss. We just brought a few odds and ends we thought you might use." Mrs. Jollie handed me a bulging basket covered with a brightly patterned tea cloth. "Miss Briggs and I've not been inside Highdrift. Looks right nice in the daytime."

"Please come in," I said. "There's not much to see. It's small and still very primitive."

"The kitchen don't look half bad," said Mrs. Jollie. "Nice cooker over by the chimney, sink under the window, and a nice big table."

"Oh yes," said Miss Briggs in a soft tone, "any place that is truly your own is wonderful. You are very fortunate."

"You're right, and I am grateful; it's just that my work is in London, and I feel a bit of a shirker being here and fixing the house. I'm enjoying the work, though, and I think Father is too. He and Mr. Ott seem to be getting on very well. Come into the living area," I said as I opened the kitchen door.

"That Ott, I see he's been cleaning chimneys again," said Mrs. Jollie, pointing to the gaping hole.

"Yes, he has, with Father's help. They make a dangerous pair, I think," I said with a laugh.

Miss Briggs smiled but seemed a bit vague and preoccupied. She stood in the middle of the living room, looking at the dark, square roughhewn beams and the large windows with their

myriad of small diamond-shaped, leaded panes. "What a lovely .
. ." as she turned around and caught sight of the wicker hamper
over at the foot of the stairs, she fell silent and gripped my arm
like a vice.

I cried, "Miss Briggs, please, you're hurting me!" The secretary
immediately let go and then burst into tears. Mrs. Jollie grabbed
the sobbing woman around the shoulders and shepherded her
back towards the kitchen, sitting her down at the large table.

"There, there, Mary," Mrs. Jollie crooned as she patted the
secretary's back. "Everything's all right; take it easy now. Miss
Alberta, maybe a glass of water."

"Of course, and I'll put on the kettle for tea."

I got Miss Briggs some water and then busied myself filling
the teakettle at the sink hand pump.

Miss Briggs made hiccoughing apologies. "I am so sorry; I feel
a complete fool. I saw that big hamper at the foot of the stairs,
and it looked so much like the one Flora . . ." The secretary
reached out a shaky hand for the glass of water sitting beside
her; she took one sip and started coughing. I rushed over and
patted her sharply on the back. Miss Briggs took a deep breath
and then slumped onto the table, her head buried in her arms.

"Oh, Mary," Mrs. Jollie said as she reached for the woman. I
stopped her, "Mrs. Jollie, the kettle's boiling. Could you help
me, please?"

Mrs. Jollie got up, and we walked toward the spirit stove.
She took the kettle off the boil and set it on the stovetop. I
whispered, "Maybe we should let her alone. Come with me out
on the terrace for a bit." We made a singular pair, one tall and
slender, the other short and stocky; we headed out of the chilly
kitchen into the spring sunshine where Sabin and I had been
not long before and took a seat on the low stone balustrade that

encircled the terrace.

"It was that trunk that done it," Mrs. Jollie stated. "Mary was feeling more the thing today. She wants to leave Lanmorech and go to London and was going to ask you to help her enroll as a VAD, poor soul."

"My father and I would be more than pleased to help Miss Briggs in any way we can," I said. "I don't think the local constabulary will let her leave just yet, though. I got the impression that Saben Best needs to talk to everyone here that knew Flora Hicks. Miss Briggs knew her, didn't she?"

"The girl was staying at Penrose House, so we all had made her acquaintance. But I couldn't say how well anyone knew her," said Mrs. Jollie.

Halting footsteps echoed across the kitchen floor. Mary Briggs stood in the doorway, her eyes and nose bright red from weeping and her hair all disheveled. "I'm feeling more myself now; might I have a cup of tea?" I started to rise.

"No, Miss Alberta, let me," Mrs. Jollie said. "Mary, come out into the sunshine and sit down." Mrs. Jollie trotted into the kitchen to make the tea.

"I appreciate your letting me bawl like that," said Miss Briggs as she sat on the ledge. "At Penrose House, they've really been very good to me, but I'm just Miss Briggs, self-contained secretary, in command of herself at all times. I just needed a good cry, I guess."

I reached across the rough stone ledge and patted her cold, clammy hand. "Sometimes we all need a good cry." We sat in silence until an automobile pulled up at the side of the house. Doors slammed, and the voices of Father and Mr. Ott, raised in a friendly argument with Saben Best playing referee, floated across the yard. I jumped up and sprinted across the terrace to head the men off so Miss Briggs would have a little time to compose herself.

"So, how did you do?" I asked as I grabbed Father's elbow and gently steered him along the driveway to the front of the house.

"Fine dear, fine. Ott here has a brother that owns the mercantile. He just walked in and grabbed a few things to fix the chimney. Then we went over next door to the *Tin Whistle*; Ott's cousin, Humphrey, runs that little establishment. We got cleaned up there and got some lunch."

Father and I walked up the stone steps and entered the house, followed by Mr. Ott and Saben. "You did a grand job of setting the room to rights, Miss Alberta," said Mr. Ott as he stood, hands-on-hips, surveying the room. "We'll get that hole patched in a jiffy."

Father and Mr. Ott drifted over to the fireplace and were deep in discussion. Saben walked up to me and handed over a small paper sack. "Here, I thought you might need something for lunch and didn't figure there'd be much about the house yet."

I stood still for a minute, mouth open, "Why thanks, that was very thoughtful of you." Just then, Mrs. Jollie came out of the kitchen, nodded to Saben, and bent to whisper in my ear. "All right, Mrs. Jollie, that might be best. Tell Miss Briggs I'll make some inquiries and be in touch. And thank you so much for the basket." Mrs. Jollie turned and went quietly back into the kitchen. Saben watched her leave and then turned to me with a questioning look. I held up my hand and went down the hall. I made sure the ladies had gone and then beckoned Saben into the kitchen.

"What was that all about?" Saben asked as he pulled out a chair and sat down.

I let out a sigh, "Oh, it's Miss Briggs. She is seriously shaken up, understandably so, and wants Father and me to help her apply for the Red Cross. She wants to leave Lanmorech and go to London; I can't say I blame her." I walked over to the wall cupboard and took out a plate; I opened the bag Saben had brought and smelled the warm, crusty pasty. I turned and relit the spirit stove and grabbed Mrs. Jollie's towel-covered basket. Next, I rinsed out two cups and saucers and set them on the table. I slid Saben's empty teacup towards him and sat down opposite. I reached across to take the tea cloth off the basket to expose the goodies from the Manor.

"Mmm, looks good. Scones, strawberry jam, clotted cream. Just like before the war," Saben said.

There was a bump at the swinging door, and Father came through the kitchen carrying a metal bucket. "Need some water," he said as he pumped the handle at the kitchen sink.

"Do the mixing outside, please. We don't want any of that stuff on the floor," I called after Father's retreating back. The teakettle whistled, and I jumped up.

"Now, about Miss Briggs?" Saben said.

I took a quick bite of the pasty. "Mmm, so good," I mumbled. "Well, Miss Briggs is an emotional mess; she sat here bawling just before you arrived. I mentioned that the matter of Flora's death might slow up any departures but told her Father and I would do what we could for her."

"Flora's death will more than slow some departures, I'm afraid. It looks like the investigation is being taken out of my hands," Saben said. "Some inspector is being sent from London to handle things."

"From London? But I thought since she died here . . ."

"That's just it; Miss Hicks didn't die here. It's been determined

73

that she died late Friday night. We have tried to reconstruct Flora's movements, and we are pretty certain she came down on the *Night Riviera*. Or, to be more accurate, was killed on the *Night Riviera*."

"But Father and I took that train."

"Yes, I know," Saben said.

Scotland Yard Takes Over

Father and I stared at the flicker of flames in the fireplace. "Repairing that chimney was backbreaking, but it turned out nice, don't you think?"

"Hmm…, Father, there's something I need to show you; it's been worrying me all day." I rose from the hard kitchen chair and went to the staircase. I had carried the other boxes and suitcases upstairs, but the wicker trunk remained. "Do you know how this got here?"

"Why it came from the train station with the other cases, I would assume, I'm not sure," Father said, with a questioning look. He slowly stood, put his hand to the small of his back, and sucked in his breath. He limped over and reached to undo the latch on the large wicker trunk. The lid creaked as father opened it and leaned it against the wall. "That's not mine. That is not my trunk nor my belongings. What's going on here?"

"What's going on here is, somehow, we have ended up with someone else's trunk. I did a cursory examination of the contents, which belong to a youngish woman by the looks of them, and I'm scared to death that they are Flora Hicks'."

"Why in the world should this trunk be Flora Hicks'?"

"Well, we were all three passengers on the same train; our trunks would have traveled in the same baggage car. Also, Flora was one passenger that would not have picked up her trunk nor complained when it didn't arrive."

"Oh my word, that's true. So where is my trunk? You know I packed my books and pictures …."

"Father, you don't seem to understand the seriousness of this situation. If Flora's trunk is here, then your trunk may well be at the police station."

"No, there's…, no, it couldn't be." Father lifted his hand up his forehead and limped back to the fire. He sat with a jolt on the ladder-backed chair, leaned back, and closed his eyes.

I shut and latched the trunk's lid, went to Father, and took his work-roughened hand in mine, "We'll contact Saben. He'll know what to do."

The next morning, in bed with my eyes closed, I listened to the birds chatter and chirp. I stretched and sighed in contentment and started to make a mental list of what to do at Highdrift. Then my pleasure melted away. Today, Father and I had to speak with Saben. I rose from the bed, took two steps to the window, and lifted the casement. Usually, by leaning way out, I could see the tip of the cobalt and turquoise bay. But today, a morning mist made it difficult to tell where the sky ended and the sea began. As I popped back through the window, I caught a faint whiff of smoke. Father must be kindling fires. He was so proud of that clean chimney. I slipped on my fuzzy yellow robe and headed for the bathroom. "Good morning Father; how did you sleep?" I called from the bottom stair.

"Pretty fitfully, I'm afraid," Father answered. "My mind kept running over the various scenarios for today's interview with the local constabulary. Why I am so worried, I don't know, but there it is. I have this knot in my stomach and a feeling of dread I can't shake. Did we ever have any connection with this Miss Hicks?"

"I don't believe either of us ever actually met her, but she did write a note once and try to arrange a meeting. She even suggested a visit to the Vicarage. We just never managed it; we always seemed to miss one another. It was odd, really."

Father heaved a heavy sigh, "I just want to forget about all this and putter around Highdrift. Forget about the war, about poor Miss Hicks, about the chaplaincy, everything. That's very unvicarlike of me, I suppose."

"Yes, but very human, and I must admit I feel the same way. Highdrift is so peaceful you want to settle in, pull up the drawbridge and never deal with the turbulence outside."

Father raised his eyebrows in inquiry, "You feel that too?"

"Yes, I definitely do."

"Well, since that isn't possible, we'd better do our civil and Christian duty. The sooner we get this ghastly business over, the better I'll feel."

After I had bathed and dressed, Father and I faced each other over the highly scrubbed kitchen table. He scooted the food around on his plate and had hardly eaten a bite. I couldn't eat either. Father caught my eye and shook his head. "Should we give up? Let's get this over and have a nice lunch at the *Tin Whistle*."

We retraced our journey of the previous day. Along the country lane, past the bay, now obscured by morning fog, and then up the twisty main street of the picturesque little village of Lanmorech. The Town Hall and Civic Building housed the local police station and jail. They sat neat and tidy just off the main square in a building of grayish stone with faded blue trim. Father opened the front door and motioned for me to precede him into the dim, cool entryway. I crossed to the reception desk manned by a middle-aged woman with dark, wavy hair. Her pince-nez glasses hung from a long black ribbon, and the gaze that pierced me seemed familiar. I opened my mouth to introduce myself, but the receptionist raised her hand and said, with a slight foreign accent, "I know who you are, we have met before, and this handsome man must be your Father." Her "R" rolled with a hint of flirtation. The woman stood and held out her hand just as Saben entered the anteroom.

He stopped short in surprise, "Vicar Holdaway and Miss Alberta Holdaway," Saben said in an overly loud voice as he stepped aside to gesture to the short, stout little man behind him, "this is Inspector Blodgett from Scotland Yard."

Father stepped forward and put out his hand, "Nice to meet you, sir."

After a brief hesitation, the inspector shook it. "Hm… speak of the devil."

Father gave a sharp intake of breath at Inspector Blodgett's greeting. Saben and I both leaped into the breach, speaking in a rush at the same time.

"Can I help you with…?"

"Saben, can we speak…?"

We stood frozen and embarrassed. The receptionist stepped in to ask the inspector if she could talk with him and very forcibly made it impossible for him to refuse. Relieved, Saben said, "Excuse me for a moment Inspector, while I speak to the Holdaways." The inspector frowned, displeased, but he could do nothing to stop the conference without being blatantly rude. Saben led us to his office. "We need to make this quick," whispered Saben immediately after closing his door. "The inspector went through the wicker hamper and found some items that link both of you with Flora Hicks."

"What!" exploded Vicar Holdaway, "that's impossible!"

Saben held up his hand, "Let me finish. He found some letters written to you, Vicar Holdaway. But also in the hamper were some of the Penrose Pearls, worth a small fortune which would tend to implicate the Penrose household as well."

"And," said Inspector Blodgett as he opened the office door, "all of you were on the *Night Riviera*. I suppose the best way to proceed is to get a statement from you both as to your whereabouts Friday, May 15th, from midnight, when the *Night Riviera* left Paddington Station, to 8 a.m. when you arrived at Penzance."

"I am sorry, Inspector, but I must protest," said Father. "There is no way that my daughter, nor myself for that matter, had anything to do with this tragedy. Why Alberta was unwell in our cabin recovering from an accident at the train station just before boarding."

"Is that correct, Miss Holdaway?" asked the inspector.

"Yes, I was in the cabin most of the time," I heard the hesitation in my voice, so I rushed to explain. "The cabin had a washbasin but no commode, so I did leave the cabin once."

"And do you know the exact time of your absence?"

"Around 2 a.m. I felt dizzy and unwell and slept on and off the whole trip."

"And was your father in the cabin with you the entire journey?"

"Why I, I'm not…, no, not the entire time. As I said, I slept."

"Is that correct, Vicar Holdaway?"

"Now look here, Inspector, where is all this going to take us? Obviously, we were not together every second of an eight-hour train journey."

Inspector Blodgett walked over to Father and stood very close. He raised his arm and started poking Father in the chest to emphasize every word he uttered. "Now listen, Vicar, we're dealing with murder here. Just because you wear a collar around your neck does not give you immunity from investigation. It may give you a pass to stay in this nice cozy little village for the duration of the war, but it cuts no ice with me!"

There was dead silence. Father turned his back on the inspector. It was as if a switch was thrown, and all Father's energy seeped away. He turned to leave the stuffy little office, stooped and defeated. As he was about to close the door, he looked back, "See that Alberta makes it home all right, please, Saben."

The inspector moved to go after Father, but Saben grabbed the sleeve of his jacket, "Let the man be. I'll talk to him when I take Alberta home."

"This is very irregular, Constable Best. I need a free hand with this investigation. I'm sick to death of these shirkers telling me how to do my job."

"Now listen, Inspector," Saben said," I want to give you every courtesy and full cooperation, but I will not stand for bullying by anyone for any reason. This is not London. We do things differently here, and if the community feels someone is being treated unfairly, you will get no cooperation from anyone. I suggest you let me arrange a meeting with the Penroses and the Holdaways, and we can get the timetable of activity aboard the train pinned down as much as possible and see where that leaves us."

The inspector let out a huge sigh and stood still, head bent deep in thought. "There's wisdom in that suggestion, I agree." The inspector shook Saben's hand, nodded to Alberta, and left the room.

"Whew, what was that about?" I whispered as I watched the inspector's retreating form.

"Inspector Blodgett's son went missing at Verdun," Saben said quietly. "Well, come on, let's drive up to Penrose House to set up some sort of meeting, and then I'll take you home." Saben walked out of the office into the foyer. As I followed behind, I noticed an uncharacteristic droop of his shoulders and the pronouncement of his limp. Saben stopped by the front desk to tell the receptionist where he was going. The woman rushed up, put her hands on Saben's face, and looked deep into his eyes. Then I recognized her; it was Morvah, the woman at the church fete.

"My darling," she said, her voice full of concern, "You are exhausted; go home and get some rest. I will be home early tonight and fix you a relaxing tisane."

Saben smiled and kissed Morvah on the cheek, "Mother, you worry too much."

"Always, no matter what I say to him, it's the same, Mother, you worry too much." She walked back to her desk, shaking her head.

I kept quiet until we were outside on the pavement, "Morvah, is your Mother?"

"Yes," Saben replied, "Morvah is my mother." We walked

shoulder to shoulder up the pavement to where a green "Model T" Ford sat. Saben reached inside the car, pulled the spark lever up, set the throttle lever down to one quarter, and switched the battery to "off." Then he walked to the front of the car and pulled out the choke ring. I slid behind the steering wheel and waited for Saben to turn the crank. He gave the crank one turn, then another. Saben had a startled expression when he lifted his head and saw me in the driver's seat. I switched the battery on. Then the young constable gave the engine another crank, and the automobile rumbled to life. Saben walked to the car's passenger side, opened the door, and climbed in. I released the choke, put the car in neutral, took the handbrake off, kept my right foot on the brake pedal, and slowly adjusted the throttle. Next, I pushed the clutch pedal to the floor, let off the brake, and pulled out from the curb in low gear.

We puttered down the bumpy cobbled lane at a sedate pace. I flashed Saben a smile as I pulled out onto the more wide-open roadway, adjusted the throttle, and put the car into high gear. I clenched the steering wheel and kept my eyes glued to the empty, hard-pan road, determined to demonstrate my incredible driving prowess. I was surprised Saben allowed me to drive without a murmur. I stole a glance at my passenger; he sat with his head bobbing against the car's door frame. I leaned forward and quickly looked at Saben's face; he was fast asleep. I smiled, then leaned back and relaxed. I unclenched my hands, let out my breath, and looked across the startlingly blue bay. The early morning fog had lifted, and the sparkling azure water lay framed by a crescent of sand.

A feeling of guilt began to intrude on my thoughts. I was enjoying this country life in Lanmorech too well. The war seemed a long way off. The sooner I got back to London and

Devonshire House, back to work, the better.

The old rowan tree was on my right; the turn for Highdrift was just around the bend. I put the Model T into low gear and carefully turned onto the narrow lane I had walked down this morning with Father. I eased onto the small driveway next to the house, pushed the brake pedal, and pulled the hand lever. The car shuddered to a stop, and Saben jerked awake.

"Sorry, I flunked, stopping."

Saben yawned and stretched, "You should have gone straight up the hill to Penrose House; you were doing great."

"How could you tell?"

"I was just resting my eyes," Saben protested, "I wasn't sleeping."

"If you were awake, why didn't you tell me not to turn off the main road?"

"Why did you come to Highdrift?" Saben said, not answering the question.

"I wanted to make sure Father got home all right, and I don't know the way to Penrose House."

"Well, now you and your father, if he's here, can come up the hill with me. Penrose House is just a few miles up the main road."

I opened the car door, stepped on the running board, and then climbed down from the car, giving the shiny forest-green metal an affectionate pat.

Saben shut the passenger door with a click. "I smell smoke."

A gray curl rose over the roof line. I ran down the drive and beyond the stone patio. Father leaned on a weather-beaten shovel at the edge of the small fruit orchard, staring into a fire coming from a small pile of smoldering leaves and branches. I put a hand up to still my pounding heart and heaved a sigh of relief at seeing his tousled hair and rumpled, moth-eaten gray sweater.

The vicar looked up confused, "Alberta, what's the matter?"

"Nothing, not a thing, Father. I was just being silly."

"You thought I'd stop by *The Tin Whistle* after my encounter with the inspector, I expect," Father said. "Well, to be quite honest, it crossed my mind and required great intestinal fortitude and a few prayers to avoid that pitfall. However, as you can see, I prevailed against my weakness. Instead, I am trying not to burn down this lovely old orchard. I didn't even notice the fruit trees before; the weeds and vines were so dense. Look, Saben, plums, apples, pears; the birds will steal all the cherries, but with a little judicious pruning, the trees could be brought back to a respectable production."

"Oh, how lovely to have fresh fruit right out the backdoor. I could make jam and preserves; maybe dry some fruit on those old screens in the shed." I was so happy to see Father home safely and enthusiastic about life at Highdrift; it was easy to forget my recent resolve to get back to London immediately.

Police at Penrose

I pulled my trench coat tight and grabbed the plaid wool lap robe on the backseat to spread over my legs. The sun shone, but the breeze that blew through the car was brisk as Saben drove up the hill to Penrose House. The road followed the bay most of the way, then turned inland and began a steady climb through terrain that was a study of contrasts. The rough and rugged outcroppings of stone and wind-bent trees along the coast gave way to a sheltered valley. The valley was lush and green, with fields ringed by gorse and stones in the distance. After driving a couple of miles, I saw a high wall of the same bluish-gray stone as Highdrift. Saben abruptly turned off the lane to pass through two massive wrought iron gates. The gates, each emblazoned by a wildly stylized "P," stood wide open. We slipped from a sky full of spring sunshine and cool breezes to a canopy of interlocking branches that created a sunless oppressive gloom. Then suddenly, the trees opened up. Within the cup of a small valley was a perfect medieval manor house, stone walls, and battlements ready to fend off the foreign or threatening. The car rattled incongruously past the large square gatehouse and stopped.

I climbed out of the car. As I walked to where Father stood, my feet crunched in the thick gravel. I took his hand. "Magnificent isn't it?" he said as we looked out over the large expanse of lawn down to the sea. "And look back there at the terraces that run up the hill," Father pointed.

"Not in as pristine condition as before the war, I'm afraid," said the gentleman in worn tweeds, coming down the stairs.

"Hello, Penrose," Father said, holding out his hand. He pulled me forward, "let me introduce my daughter Alberta."

"Nice to meet you, Alberta. Aren't you lovely? You look so much like your dear mother." Lord Penrose took my arm and put it in the crook of his own. He led me up the steps toward the tremendous arched door, which slowly opened. As if through magic, an elderly butler appeared, "Bing, please tell my wife, Saben, and the Holdaways have arrived. Tell her Ambrose and Alberta will wait on her in the upstairs sitting room when Saben has finished the interview." Without a word, in total silence, the butler departed. Lord Penrose smiled at me, "I don't know how he does that."

I had to laugh, and I felt my tension ease. "I had no idea. Binky always calls it the 'rock pile.'"

"Well, she's accurate if not flattering," said Lord Penrose. "This is the oldest portion of the house and has been left relatively untouched by modern comfort. We live in the rear wing added in 1750." The front entryway was larger than the whole of Highdrift, with floors of Carrara marble and oak walls, blackened with age and covered with weapons and shields. There was a fireplace at one end large enough to hold a whole ox, and an incredible chandelier hung above us that, in an earlier day, must have held a hundred candles.

Our footsteps echoed as Lord Penrose ushered us into the sitting room. Saben steered me to an inconspicuous spot in the oversize wing-back chair before the French patio doors. Saben had asked that I take notes of this question-and-answer session. Dowager Lady Beatrice Penrose was first.

"Lady Penrose, as you know, I am here to get an account from everyone in this household who traveled from London on the *Night Riviera* on the 15th of May, Thursday last," Saben said.

"You know perfectly well that I traveled on that train. I boarded early at about 10 p.m., as was my habit, and stayed in the cabin for most of the trip, then retired as soon as we got underway. I always sleep very soundly on the train, as my maid-cum-secretary, Briggs, gives me a sleeping powder. I know nothing about this awful business and highly object to you questioning the servants."

"Why would you object to my questioning the servants?" Saben asked.

"Some of them are highly impressionable and given to fancies and are not what I would call reliable witnesses." With that, Lady Penrose stood up, turned on her heel, and left the room; the interview was over.

As soon as his mother left, Lord Penrose entered the sitting room. He greeted Saben, Father, and myself and then went over to the fireplace and stood with his hands clenched behind his back, staring into the fire.

"Lord Penrose, I'm sorry to invade your home, but this seems easiest for everyone," Saben explained.

"I quite understand, Saben; I . . ." There was a discreet tap at the door, and Lady Olivia Penrose came slowly into the room. I had not met Lady Olivia; I was surprised at how vibrant and young she was. She wore her shiny auburn hair in a sleek chignon and a light lawn dress with dropped waist whose fullness hid her advanced pregnancy.

Lord Penrose rushed to her side, "Olivia, my dear, what are you doing? I told you I would speak to the police for you. There's no need for you to subject yourself to this questioning."

"Bertram, I want to do what I can for poor Flora." Lord Penrose put his arm around his wife and guided her to the sofa. Then Lady Olivia put her arm on the back of the couch and lowered herself stiffly with her husband's help. She heaved a sigh of relief and settled into the plush softness. Lord Penrose grabbed a throw pillow and placed it at the small of his wife's back; a look of such delight passed between them that I was embarrassed to witness it. I looked away and caught Saben's eye. I felt my cheeks burn and looked back down at my notepad. "Excuse the interruption," said Lady Penrose, "but I felt I had to join in this conversation. I was responsible for bringing the poor girl into this house, and I think I may have been the last one to see her alive."

"What, Olivia, my dear, what are you saying?" exclaimed her husband.

"Bertram, I know you want to shield me from any unpleasantness, but keeping this pent-up inside is making me ill. I must tell Saben everything I have seen, everything that has gone on since we heard about that blasted pearl drive!" Lord Penrose walked back over to the fireplace with an air of defeat and leaned his hand against the mantel. He stood silently for a moment, then sat by his wife. He brought her hand to his lips in the act of pure adoration and nodded.

"Alberta, I hope I may call you Alberta," said Lady Penrose as she smiled across the room at me, where I sat ensconced in the wing-backed chair, "make sure to get all this down. I'm going to tell this once, and then I'm going upstairs to relax and forget about this dreadful business and this ghastly war until my baby comes."

"This all started for Bertram and me a year ago. We had wanted to start a family but had been unsuccessful. I feared it was all my fault, so I consulted a Harley Street specialist without telling my husband. Bertram is very generous and pays every bill without a murmur, but I had no funds to use without his knowledge. I went to stay with an old school chum of mine in London, and she suggested I sell a piece of my jewelry, or rather she would sell it for me. So, that's what I did. I sold the pearls Bertram had bought me for some birthday or other. Pearls are my birthstone, but they're cold unlucky things; I never wore them. I went to the specialist. He told me I was perfectly healthy. He told me, in no uncertain terms, to get off my duff and devote my time to something useful. I came down to Lanmorech to soothe my wounded pride and joined the local Red Cross auxiliary. Then someone introduced me to Flora Hicks. I worked with her here in Lanmorech on a few Red Cross fundraisers. She was a quiet, shy, bumbling sort of person, always saying and doing the wrong thing. I felt sorry for her. I took her under my wing. We put together some successful fundraisers. Later, Flora went to London to British Red Cross headquarters. She was asked to organize the local Pearl collection. Of course, she called on me for help and expected me to donate. I kept making excuses and put her off. Finally, I told her what I had done. She said she would keep quiet about it." Olivia Penrose plucked her linen handkerchief from the cuff of her dress, dabbed her forehead, then continued.

Right about this time, Flora began regular trips to London. I assumed they were Red Cross-related, but now I believe she saw a man. She had a profound behavior change and became depressed and distracted. I was concerned about her and invited her to stay at Penrose House. She was beginning to receive pearls as donations, and I offered to let her keep them in our safe. At this time, Bertram suggested I donate my pearls, but I just couldn't admit to him that the pearls had been sold. Flora said she knew someone who could get me a good fake strand, which I could substitute. This seemed to be a harmless enough solution, so I agreed. That was about two weeks before the church sale."

At this point, Lady Penrose paused; she looked over at her husband. "Dear, do you think it would be possible for you to ask Bing to bring us tea?"

"Of course, my dear," Lord Penrose said. He leaped like a Jack-in-the-box from the sofa and hurried from the room.

Lady Penrose watched him go and made sure he was out of earshot before she said in a quiet tone, "You see why I must keep things from him? He is so excited about this baby and worries so. Now, where was I?" Lady Penrose looked over at me.

"You agreed to the pearl substitution, which was two weeks before the fete," I said.

"Yes, as it happened, we were all going up to London; we needed to shut up the London house. Bertram insisted on my moving down to Lanmorech for the duration of the war, and he would stay at his London club on the days he was needed at the War Ministry. I believe Flora traveled down on the same train, but I did not see her. On Tuesday, Flora sent me a note telling me the pearls would be delivered to me the next day. I was to meet her at the little tea shop on Harley Street, across from Doctor Beagle's office. Wednesday, I went to my doctor's appointment alone and waited for Flora at the appointed place. She did not appear. Instead, a tall young man in an ill-fitting suit came up behind me and slid a small wrapped box onto the table. I turned around as quickly as I could manage, but I could only see his retreating back."

Olivia Penrose paused, and we heard the rattle of the tea cart as it came down the hallway. Lord Penrose and the housekeeper, Mrs. Ott, appeared with the refreshments. Saben suggested we take a break, so I laid aside my notebook, stood up, and discreetly stretched my cramped limbs. "Shall I pour?" I asked.

"Indeed not," said Beatrice Penrose as she swept into the room. "It's unlucky to pour tea in another's home."

"Oh, poppycock," said Lord Penrose. "Here, let me be Mother," he said as he sat down before the tea cart. The brief respite for tea and the appearance of Dowager Lady Penrose effectively concluded Olivia Penrose's statement. Her husband hustled her off upstairs and proceeded with his narrative.

"First, I must state that I had no idea about the pearls and would not have cared if I had. Olivia's possessions are her own to do with as she pleases. I was not happy about her deception, and it was odd for Flora even to suggest such a thing; most uncharacteristic." Lord Penrose got up from the couch, paced back and forth, then went back to the fire and turned his back to us. "About the journey down on the train, I swear there was nothing untoward. Mother, Olivia, and the servants were all as usual. I had a nice visit with Ambrose, Vicar Holdaway, in my stateroom. We had a couple of drinks, and he went back to check on Alberta, who, I understand, had an accident at Paddington Station. That's all I know."

Saben looked at Father, his eyebrows raised. Father nodded

in agreement, "Penrose is right. There was nothing unusual as far as I could tell." He thought for a moment, then looked over at me, "Except for Alberta's accident, of course. She thought she was pushed deliberately. I pooh-pooed that idea at the time, but …" All eyes turned toward me, hunched over in the wing-backed chair, scribbling like mad. I lifted my head, "All I can tell is I felt a hard shove. No one said 'sorry' or 'excuse me.' I just lay there on the cold floor; people either gawked or moved around me."

"And some woman helped," Father said.

"That's right; she was in uniform; I got the impression she worked at the aid station. She wore a large hat; I was dizzy and can't remember what she looked like. Could it have been Flora?" I felt panic rise; my pulse began to pound. I put my hand up to my temple.

"All right," Father said as he stood, "that is enough. Alberta has been questioned by that inspector already."

Saben nodded in agreement. "Let us have a quick word with the servants, and I'll drop you two home. Alberta, can you bear to take a few more statements?"

I nodded without saying anything. I rubbed my tight neck muscles, then stood and followed Constable Best. Mrs. Ott met us at the study door and led us down the dark-paneled hallway to a flight of well-lighted stairs, which plunged downward. The thick carpet that dressed each tread muffled our progress into the servants' domain. I expected the dank, dark below-stairs of the Gothic novel. The stifling luxury was absent, yet Penrose House provided its caretakers with bright, clean, efficient surroundings. As we neared the end of the corridor, I heard voices; rumbles and quarrelsome chatter filtered through a partially closed door. Then someone spat out the word "gypsy," more grumbling, "damned cheek if you ask me."

I heard the sharp intake of Mrs. Ott's breath and felt Sabin stiffen beside me. The housekeeper quickly entered the sitting room. "Detective Best is here to ask you a few questions. Lord Penrose expects your full cooperation and courtesy in this matter." There were eight people seated around the heavy oak table. I recognized Mrs. Jollie, Miss Briggs, and Bing, the stiff and stern butler. The others were new to me.

"I need to speak only to those of you who were on the *Night Riviera* last week with the Penroses," Saben said. Bing, two girls in maid's uniforms, and one man dressed as chauffeur stood up to beat a hasty retreat. "Now, Miss Holdaway will take down statements detailing what you experienced on the night of Friday, May 15th."

I took brief statements from Mrs. Jollie, Miss Briggs, Mr. Pelham, Lord Penrose's secretary, Stapleton, his Lordship's valet, and Norris, Lady Olivia Penrose's maid. Each statement was the same; "No, the servants were not together the entire train trip. There was the normal amount of coming and going. No one noticed anything unusual. No one had seen Flora Hicks." I finished my note-taking and closed the cover of my pad. Saben stood up and turned to speak to the housekeeper in a tone loud enough for everyone in the room to hear. "Mrs. Ott, if anyone comes to you with more information or questions, please contact me at any time. Scotland Yard is involved in this investigation because of the seriousness and location of this crime. We are determined to solve this quickly. Thank you all for your help."

Saben stood by the door and waited for me to precede him. Saben gently grabbed my elbow and steered me down the corridor to the tradesman's entrance. "The car's right out here.

We'll go 'round front and pick up the Vicar." I climbed in the backseat, leaned my head back, and closed my eyes. "That was very helpful, Alberta; thank you," Saben said as he drove around the sweeping gravel driveway.

"Helpful? They all said the same thing; nothing happened."

"Ah, but that was not the point of this little dance. Now the household knows that if they don't deal with me on this matter, they will have to deal with Inspector Blodgett. Mark my words; I will have a steady stream of visitors from this little episode. You see, I may be part gypsy, but I'm also a local. Blodgett's considered a foreigner." Saben pulled up to the front steps of Penrose House. Lord Penrose shook Father's hand as Bing opened the car door. Father got in, and we started back to Highdrift in thoughtful silence.

It wasn't until we passed the old Rowan tree that any of us spoke. "Did you find out anything downstairs?" Father asked.

Saben shook his head, "Nothing new, just confirmation no one noticed anything unusual during that train journey."

I leaned forward and rested my chin on the front seat, "What I found interesting was that everyone agrees Flora was a happy, uncomplicated person until a month ago. It seems to me the key to her death is in London. There may be no Lanmorech connection at all."

"Mmm, I disagree. I think this is about those pearls...." Saben broke off abruptly as he pulled up behind a black sedan parked in the driveway next to Highdrift. "That looks like Blodgett's automobile." I hung back a moment as Father and Saben got out of the car and headed toward the house. Inspector Blodgett and another man stepped out of the front porch's shadows. A dizziness came over me, and I decided to avoid the men and go around to the kitchen door at the back. I heard a murmur of voices as Father greeted the officers and invited them in.

It was cool and dim on the back patio. I hated to go into the house. Inspector Blodgett meant trouble, I was sure. I reached under the flowerpot on the windowsill for the key and unlocked the door. The instant I stepped in, I heard raised voices. I held my breath and listened; the stone and stucco walls made eavesdropping impossible. I pushed the kitchen door open, walked a few steps down the hall, and entered the front room.

The scene was worse than I expected, Saben had Father's arms pinned behind his back, and they were struggling. Inspector Blodgett stood before them with a pair of handcuffs, "I didn't expect I would need these. Just goes to show you my first impression was right."

I swear I saw Saben loosen his grip on Father. Father pushed Saben away and took a wild swing at Inspector Blodgett. I heard a distinct crunch and saw blood spurting from the inspector's nose. Next, I saw tiny white dots, I fell, and everything went black.

The Dowager, Morvah and Me

When I came to, I lay in my bed, sapped and groggy, my eyes puffy and full of grit. I threw my arm over my face to block the memories that trickled back. It was like replaying a scene from one of those new silent movies. The inspector from Scotland Yard arrests the father for murder while the ineffectual daughter stands there wringing her hands and collapses. I sat bolt-upright in bed. Waves of dizziness flowed over me. I leaned back against the headboard, closed my eyes, and sat still for a moment.

From downstairs, the mummer of voices followed by muffled laughter reached me. Laughter! My heart pounded; I couldn't believe my ears. Fear mixed with anger as I searched for some sort of bludgeon. My eyes fell on my trusty umbrella. I gingerly tip-toed out the door and down the hall. I stopped at the head of the stairs, lifted my umbrella in a threatening position, and yelled, "Who's there?"

"You needn't yell the house down," said a familiar crotchety voice.

Then came the sprightly click-clack of high heels, and Morvah Best looked up at me from the foot of the stairs. I lowered my weapon and walked warily down to them.

"What are you two doing here?"

Morvah held out her arms, "Oh, my darling girl." That was all it took. I walked into her embrace and sobbed. Morvah patted my back and soothed me like a small child. I got hold of myself and stepped back. A wrinkled hand appeared over Morvah's shoulder. It proffered a lavender-scented lawn handkerchief with the embroidered initials "BP." Mortified, I looked up into the bulging light blue eyes of Dowager Lady Beatrice Penrose.

I accepted the hankie in the spirit offered, left Morvah's arms, went to Lady Beatrice, and enfolded her in my own. "Thank you both," I said, my voice muffled by Lady Beatrice's ample bosom. "What am I going to do?"

"We are going to put our heads together and find out who did this," said Lady Beatrice with absolute conviction. The Dowager Duchess and Morvah led me into the kitchen and sat me down at the table. 'Now," said Lady Beatrice in a matter-of-fact tone, "we must come up with a plan of attack."

"But how do I attack Scotland Yard?" I cried. "Don't you understand, they put handcuffs on my father and led him away? That awful inspector and your son, Morvah."

Morvah reached her hand across the smooth pine tabletop and covered mine, "Yes, dear, but my son also sent us here to watch over you. He knows your father is not the guilty one."

"Then why…?"

"The investigation is in the inspector's hands. The man, blinded by his grief and distrust, misconstrued the facts. The inspector's superiors put pressure to bear for an arrest, so it pleased him to lay the murder at your father's door. Saben has protested, but Saben is a local constable of Romani heritage. Either of those circumstances would be enough to mute his voice."

"I'm afraid Morvah is correct," said Lady Beatrice. "That Inspector is a bigoted idiot, and Ambrose has behaved likewise. Assaulting an officer, really."

"I don't know that I'd put it that way," said Morvah, "but the result is the same. Ambrose is in jail."

"If Saben has no influence and has just to sit there while Father is falsely accused, what can we do about it?" I asked.

"My dear," said Lady Penrose, in her high sophisticated drawl, "sometimes the unofficial channels are the best. Especially now, during times of war. The problems of one VAD and one Vicar lose their importance in the grand scheme of things. But this is of supreme importance to us, and all three of us have our own spheres of influence, unique talents, and qualifications."

"Me, what influence can I possibly have?" I said as I placed my aching head in my hands.

Morvah got up from the kitchen table, came around behind me, and began to knead my shoulders. "You are better situated than we, Alberta. You have connections in London at the Red Cross and elsewhere, and I suspect a large part of this mystery lies there."

The massage relaxed my muscles, and I could feel some of Morvah's optimism and energy flowing through me. "You really think we could find something out ourselves?"

Lady Penrose went to the rustic dresser next to the sink and poured a small amount of clear liquid from an earthen jug. She brought it over to the table and set the glass before me, "Here, Alberta, drink this."

I looked up at Lady Beatrice with suspicion, and Morvah halted her massage, "Yes, Alberta, take a sip; it is a restorative I make from plums."

I took a small sip and felt a fruity warmth spread from my mouth to my stomach. I could feel myself relax. I took another sip; Morvah started working on my neck and gently tapped down my spine. I let out a sigh and laid my head down on the table.

"Don't put her to sleep, Morvah," said Lady Beatrice, "we have plans to make."

"I can see why you two were giggling before I came down," I said. "What is this concoction?"

"Tuica, a traditional plum brandy. I make it in the autumn every year," said Morvah. "It is used before meals to stimulate the appetite and at occasions of great celebration. Morvah went to the little makeshift buffet and refilled the two small glasses. She came over and put a bit more Tuica in my glass. "Here, Lady Beatrice, Alberta, we will seal this entente." She lifted her glass, "After bad luck follows good fortune."

A short while later, Morvah slapped her glass sharply on the table and stood, "It is time for us to go and for you to get some rest. Would you wish me to return and stay with you?"

"Oh, no, Morvah. That's not necessary. I'll be fine. I must confess, I always faint at the sight of blood. That's why I am a typist for the Red Cross instead of a nursing VAD. It was the inspector's nose; just thinking about it makes me woozy."

Lady Penrose let out a whoop of laughter, "I wish I'd been there to see it." Then she patted my hand, "I'm sorry, ma'dear; it must be the Tuica."

"Father swung wild but definitely connected. I don't suppose that will endear him to Inspector Blodgett."

"No, I don't suppose it will. But it may endear Ambrose to everyone else in Lanmorech," Lady Beatrice chuckled again.

"To Saben, especially," said Morvah. "He has wanted to do just such a thing many times."

The two women made their way to the door, "I will send a car for you so you can drive yourself to the station. Here is a train ticket. We will all meet after you return."

I stood open-mouthed, looking at the ticket in my hand, "Lady Beatrice, you are a force of nature."

"I will take that as a compliment."

"I mean it as one," I said as I gave her a quick hug.

Father in Jail

That night I couldn't sleep. I think it was extreme worry about Father and the after-effects of the Tuica. Eventually, I got up and packed for my trip to London. Later, I tried to eat breakfast. I managed to sip some tea, took one bite of toast, then gave up. I could get something on the train after I visited Father in jail.

I tidied up the kitchen, secured the house, and grabbed my trench coat. I was just about to cram on my old brown felt hat when I hesitated; the red cloche Binky had given me for my birthday lay next to it. On a whim, I chose the cloche. Before changing my mind, I shut the closet door, grabbed my suitcase waiting in the hallway, checked my purse for the train tickets, and let myself out the front door.

As promised, a gleaming automobile was waiting in the driveway. The knot in my stomach tightened. I took a deep breath and put my suitcase in the backseat. After several attempts and a grazed knuckle, I started the car and was on my way.

The morning fog shut out most of the view, making the world

eerily small and silent. I rehearsed in my mind, over and over, what I would say to Father. I drove along the bay, up the main street, and parked near the Town Hall. I walked towards the door and saw my reflection in a window. I quickly replaced my deeply etched frown with a smile, then stood there a moment gazing at my reflection. My smile looked forced; did my hat look too red? I put a hand on my stomach to calm it down and opened the Town Hall door.

I looked across the foyer and saw a subdued Morvah; she held up her hand and beckoned me over. "Hello, Miss Holdaway, may I help you?" she said as she flashed her eyes quickly sideways.

I looked over and noticed Inspector Blodgett lounging in the doorway. He straightened up and came towards me. "I'll take Miss Holdaway back to see her father, Mrs. Best," he said, his voice muffled by the large bandage on his nose. Blodgett sauntered over to me and gently took my elbow. I wanted to snatch it away and give him a good poke in the ribs, but I just stiffened, put my chin up and let him guide me down the hallway. We went to the very end.

Inspector Blodgett stopped, dropped my elbow, reached in his pocket, and pulled out a ring of keys. He stepped in front of me, unlocked and then opened the door. I spotted Father across the room, back hunched up, sitting at a table. He was unrecognizable in the rough gray prison shirt and pants as the Vicar of St. Hugh's. He stood up when he saw me and held out his hand, "Let's hope the old saying is not true," Father said with a sad smile.

"What saying?" I asked as I took his hand and leaned across the table to kiss him on the cheek.

"That clothes make the man," he laughed, his old familiar laugh.

"You're doing all right?" I said as we both sat down.

The inspector interrupted, "I'll leave you two. Just tell Brewster when you're finished; he'll let you out."

I looked at the man in a gray uniform, almost invisible against the lighter gray wall; he nodded politely. Neither Father nor I spoke until the inspector had closed the door behind him.

"I'm fine, Alberta, don't you worry about me one bit," Father lowered his voice, "Mrs. Best and Saben are being wonderful. Saben says this is just for a few days, and Mrs. Best has arranged for me to meet Arthur Hurst. Do you remember my mentioning him? He is doing marvelous work with shell shock victims at Newton Abbott's Seale Hayne in Devon. After I get out of here, I hope to go on a visit. This won't be for long, dear. How are you getting along? I hear Lady Penrose has taken you under her ample wing."

"Yes, she has. She and Morvah have been wonderful."

"But Alberta, you should go back to London, back to work. There is nothing you need do here."

"I am going to London right after I leave you this morning. I'm catching the *Riviera Express* at 10:15, but I will return in a few days. To stay."

"Alberta…,"

"There is no sense discussing it, Father!"

"When your soft hazel eyes turn to steel, I know better than to argue."

"Good, that's settled. Can I bring you anything from London?"

"No," Father answered, "I don't want you going to the vicarage. Mrs. Pewter's gone, and that Goolsby woman is there. Where are you going to stay? "

"Either with Mrs. Pewter or at the *Braxton Hotel for Working*

Women; it's close to *Devonshire House."*

"Try and stay with Mrs. Pewter if you can; I feel I've let her down. She's been a good friend for many years."

"I know, Father," I reached across the table to grab his hand. "Don't be so hard on yourself. Mrs. Pewter certainly doesn't blame you for anything."

Father bent his head, "Maybe she should."

"Don't say such things! No, there's something to all this we aren't aware of yet, something malicious."

"Well, if that's the case, stay out of it, Alberta. No asking questions, no poking around. Someone killed that poor girl, you know, and they're out there somewhere and think they are totally in the clear."

"If whoever thinks they're safe, they will certainly want to remain so."

"Or they may be emboldened by this success," said Father. He squeezed my hand. "Leave it alone, Alberta. Promise me."

I looked at my watch. "I promise I won't do anything on my own, all right?"

Father frowned and hesitated, "There's not much I can do, is there? Just be careful. Come see me the minute you return." Father looked up, "Yes, Brewster?"

"Excuse me, Vicar, time's up."

Father slowly rose from the table. I stood up as well. I kept blinking my eyes, willing myself not to cry. I looked up at Father's face and saw his eyes swim with tears. I went around the table, and he put his arms around me, patting my back, "Now, now, my dear."

I just stood there blubbering against Father's shoulder. I stepped away, reached into my coat pocket, and pulled out a hankie. I noticed the initials *BL.* "You know I've cried more this last week ..." I took a deep breath and wiped my eyes.

"Don't worry about the Vicar, Miss Holdaway; I'm takin' good care of him. He's the best chess player we've had in here for a donkey's age," said Brewster.

"I surely hope not," Father said," I haven't beaten you yet."

"But it's been a challenge, Sir, a rare challenge."

"Thank you, Brewster."

The Riviera Express

The wind blew the morning fog away and sent dirty gray waves crashing against the sandy beach. It was ten o'clock; I had fifteen minutes before the *Riviera Express* left the Penzance train depot. I stood for a minute at the quayside and watched the storm brewing. The gulls screamed high above, either in delight at the wild wind currents or dismay that the weather had driven the crowd, their primary food supply, indoors. The gusts were so intense that I could feel the spray on my face and taste salt on my lips. I stood mesmerized by the elemental to and fro.

A loud blast of steam and the *Express'* sharp whistle made me jump and brought my thoughts back to Penzance. I picked up my suitcase and walked down the wooden platform towards the train. The *Riviera Express* was beautiful, like the shiny green Chinese dragon from a book Mother read to me as a child. This dragon waited to whisk its passengers to London, it puffed and bellowed from the depths, and a tail of fourteen cars disappeared around the bend.

A woman porter in a long dark skirt and tailored jacket walked up to me and took my case; she guided me to an empty first-class compartment, helped me in, and set my case on the floor. The porteress closed and latched my door. I smiled and gave her my thanks and a very small tip. Then, with a sigh, I relaxed on the bench seat and gazed out the salt-glazed picture window.

At 10:15 exactly, the train gave a farewell whistle, and we slowly started moving. The station of steel and glass receded into the distance, and I was on my way. Even though I would have preferred to order breakfast here in my cabin, the pressure of my new alliance with Lady Penrose and Morvah caused me to bestir myself to pursue some investigation. I left my cozy compartment and gingerly walked down the corridor, sliding my hand down the chilly brass handrail. When I stepped through the connector and opened the dining car door, I was met by the low hum of voices and row upon row of tables covered in white cloths, glistening glass, and shining silver. Most tables were already full. I noted that the occupants were primarily mothers and their children, probably returning from the peace and safety of the Cornish seaside.

As I sat down, a little girl at the table opposite spoke to her mother, "Mummy, why couldn't Daddy come with us this year? He said he would be home." The mother put her arm around her daughter and leaned close, "He will be with us next time, darling," she said. The mother moistened a cloth napkin with water from her drinking glass. She wiped her daughter's face gently and then stood up to leave. Just then, the waiter came bustling down the aisle and asked the woman how their meal had been, and then he turned and smiled at me.

"Mr. Dodd?" I asked.

"Yes, miss," he studied my face for a minute, then a look of recognition crossed his features. "Miss Holdaway, are you fully recovered from your accident? How nice to see you again."

"Thank you, Mr. Dodd; I am recovered. Would it be possible to speak to you sometime during this trip? About that poor woman found in the baggage car?"

"Well, I'm not supposed to talk about that, Miss, but seeing how you were onboard that night, I'll stop by your compartment when I get the chance."

I rushed through my breakfast and hurried back down the train corridor to my compartment. I had just sat on the banquette when I heard a discreet tap on the door.

"Come in."

The door opened, and a middle-aged woman stuck her head in. "Mr. Dodd said I was to come and speak to you, Miss," the woman hesitated.

"Please come in, have a seat."

"Oh, no, Miss, I mustn't, I just have a minute, but I want you to know that I only told what I saw. I meant no harm. "

"I'm not sure what you mean."

The woman wrung her hands, bent her head, and stared at the floor; the words poured out. "I was working on the night train the Friday that girl was killed. I wasn't supposed to be near the mail car, but sometimes we sneak back there to have a smoke, like. It's at the end of the train, so no one goes there much. Well anyway, I was there and saw someone coming out of the mail car. I couldn't see his face, but his collar shined out bright as anything. It was the Vicar. I'm so sorry, Miss, but that Inspector asked me, and I had to tell."

I was shocked and didn't reply; I just sat there frozen.

"Miss?" the girl asked, "Are you all right? Shall I call Mr.

Dodd?"

I looked up at her, "Oh, ah, what was your name?"

"Martha, Martha Watkins, Miss."

"No, Martha, I'll be all right. You did the right thing, don't you worry about that. And thank you for letting me know."

"Thank you, Miss. May I go?"

"Of course, Martha, thank you." The woman beat a hasty retreat, and I just sat there.

It just didn't make sense. Father would have had no reason to go to that end of the train, and he told everyone he was with me most of the time. At least now I knew why the police arrested Father. Inspector Blodgett had an eyewitness.

Deal Street

I caught the *Bakerloo Line* train at *Paddington Station.* I disembarked and left the underground at Dover Street, only a block from Devonshire House. The sky was overcast, and the pavement shone greasily from a recent shower. The air felt muggy and oppressive.

Nothing had changed in the short time I'd been away from London. Still, men in uniform, double-decker buses, automobiles, and horse-drawn lorries bustled along Piccadilly. The massive wrought-iron gates of Devonshire House stood open. I felt like a beggar standing there with my battered suitcase. I held my head up, stuck out my chin, and walked along the crescent-shaped pavement leading to the Grand Portico.

By the time I stepped into the echoing, marbled hallway, I was perspiring. I made my heel-tapping progress toward the Grand Ballroom. It was after six o'clock, so the headquarters of the British Red Cross was largely deserted. The door to the ballroom stood open and displayed the incongruous interior.

Walls denuded of priceless paintings, massive chandeliers draped with dust cloths, like spider cocoons, hanging from the thirty-foot high coffered and gilded ceiling, and rows upon rows of wooden worktables covered in file boxes. At this time of night, only a few people occupied the desks, which ran along the sides of the cavernous room. I leaned forward to spot anyone I knew, and low and behold, there sat Binky.

I set my suitcase down with a *click,* and Binky glanced up. Our eyes met, and she shot out of her chair and came rushing down the corridor, arms open wide. "Alberta! I've just had a cable from Granny; she said to be on the lookout for you and told me about your father. Oh, Alberta, I'm so sorry. It's utterly ridiculous."

"That's what we all keep saying, but Father's still in jail." I paused for a moment to compose myself. "Your Grandmother has taken me in hand, though; she paid for my passage and sent me here to find out about Flora."

"Yes, she said as much to me as well. Granny discussed the situation with Mrs. Brodie. She gave me access to Flora's file, but I could find nothing useful. Her family is from Devon; both parents are dead, lost a brother at the Marne early in the war. She lived with her grandmother until she came to London, then started traveling around fundraising for the Red Cross."

"Where did she stay when she was here in London?" I followed Binky over to her desk. She bent over the tabletop, turned a folder towards herself, and flipped it open. I heard a slight intake of breath. Binky said, "Isn't Deal Street near St. Hugh's?"

"You see, Binky," I said, getting all choked up, "This happens every time. All these little tidbits pile up and up and bury Father alive beneath them. And before you ask, neither Father nor I ever met Flora Hicks. I'm sure of that."

Binky reached out and touched my arm. "I believe you. How can I help?"

"Come with me to Deal Street, then to St. Hugh's?" Binky didn't even take time to answer; she wrote down Flora's address, locked her papers in her drawer, plucked her coat off the nearby coat rack, and flicked off her light.

"Can we get a quick bite to eat around the corner and then take a cab to Deal Street?"

I just nodded, too choked up to answer. I picked up my suitcase and followed Binky down the hall.

"I didn't realize it was so late," Binky said as we walked down Piccadilly. "Maybe we should grab that cab over there and go to Deal Street right away." Without waiting for my reply, Binky pulled me across the street. "1650 Deal Street, please," she said to the driver. We clambered in and set off. "Now, tell me, what are we looking for in Flora's rooms, and will we even be able to gain entrance?'

"Your grandmother wrote me an official-looking letter on Penrose stationary that requests that the landlady allow me to pick up some official estate paperwork."

"And does such paperwork exist?" asked Binky.

"I have no idea. I doubt it. I'm really looking for some link to a man. Your stepmother thinks Flora recently got involved with a man here in London."

"Odd that Flora would have been secretive about it; she wasn't the type. She was a thoroughly nice person; such a shame."

"Inspector Blodgett seems to think that man was my father."

Binky let out a hoot of laughter, "Your father, the Vicar of St. Hugh, that's ridiculous! He would never, ever do anything unseemly. I can see Flora chasing him, though. He is very attractive, unattached, and exempt from war service, pretty rare these days."

"Binky, how can you? This is serious."

"Listen, Alberta; your father's in jail. I know how serious this is."

"There's a wild card in the mix as far as Father is concerned." Binky sat beside me in the cab; she raised her eyebrows but said nothing. "You know Father has never gotten over Mother's death. Then the war came, and he had a harder and harder time helping his parishioners deal with the deaths of their loved ones. Parishioners often asked him to pray for these departed souls, and he did so to give comfort when he could. The Bishop of the Anglican Church issued a severe reprimand. Then Father applied for a chaplaincy and kept doing so regularly. His requests were met with refusal after refusal. For the past few months, Father has started drinking heavily. Right before we left for Lanmorech, I found him passed out with another rejection letter near at hand."

"So the police are accusing your father of murdering Flora while in a state of drunken amnesia? Impossible," Binky said as she took my hand. "Well, count me in on the side of the angels. Here we are at Deal Street. Let's see what we can find to clear your father."

Binky paid off the cab, and we walked through the wrought-iron fence, up a small step, and knocked on the door at 1650. The porch felt chilly and damp, but the front door was a glossy black, and its brasses shone with care. We heard a sprightly clip-clop of heels, and the door opened. "May I help you?" said the woman.

Binky stepped forward and held out her hand. "I am Lady Lawanda Penrose. And you are?"

"I am Mrs. Dowd."

"So nice to meet you, Mrs. Dowd," said Binky in her most refined tone. "We have come to see Flora Hicks."

"Oh, I'm so sorry, Miss, I mean Lady Penrose, but Miss Hicks passed away suddenly. It has been a great shock. She was such a nice girl."

Binky put her hand up to her head, and she began to waver slightly. I stood there with my mouth open, watching her performance until she grabbed my arm and pinched me.

"Yeow . . . Mrs. Dowd," I cried, "May we sit down a moment."

"Yes, of course; where are my manners? Come right on into the sitting room." She led us through an arched doorway into a dark, heavily furnished room and motioned for us to sit on a brown, plush sofa. Binky reclined slightly on the floral pillows, looking decidedly unwell.

"Excuse me," Mrs. Dowd said and left the room.

"What are you doing?" I hissed.

"Mrs. Dowd will give us tea, and we can ask her about Flora. Then I will do some more official name-dropping, and she will naturally let us see Flora's room."

"I don't know."

"That's why I took over. I know you're not a Vicar's daughter for nothing. Sh, sh, sh, here she comes."

"It's so fortunate I put the kettle on before I heard your knock. A spot of tea will perk you up, miss."

"That is so kind of you, Mrs. Dowd. I'm so sorry to be such a bother." Binky paused a moment. "Can you tell me what happened to poor Flora?"

"Why I really don't know much, just what I've seen in the papers," she said as she sat in the chair opposite Binky and me. Mrs. Dowd sighed and shook her head, "I don't know what this world is coming to, a nice girl like that, doing charity work and all. Found dead in a trunk at a church fete, the papers said. It must have been someone crazy, that's all. Just goes to show you."

"Just goes to show you what, Mrs. Dowd?" I asked.

"You're much safer in London than out in the country, even with the zeppelins."

Binky and I looked at each other but said nothing; we just accepted our cups of tea and smiled at our hostess.

"Now, Mrs. Dowd, did Flora have any visitors?" Binky asked.

"Not many, as I recall. An older woman stopped by a few times to give Flora a message. And a gentleman called once."

Binky and I both leaned forward. "Can you describe them, Mrs. Dowd?"

"Well, now, the police inspector asked me the same thing. He was very impatient and rude, and I told him no. But I've been thinking about it ever since, and I do recall that she wore some kind of uniform. Not a service uniform but a plain black coat and skirt."

"How old would you say she was?"

"Oh, about my age, I'd guess, dark hair, a little taller than me. Pretty dour didn't smile at all. I tried to pass the time of day, but she treated me like a 'nosy parker.'"

I held my breath for Binky's next question. "And what about the man?"

"He was dark too, like the woman. But I never got a look at his face. He wore a hat and a long dark coat."

"What about his voice? Could you tell how old he was?" I asked.

"Oh, I don't know. All I remember is he seemed nervous. He stopped here to drop Flora off, and they were whispering here on the porch so that I couldn't hear, but I think they were arguing about something. When they heard me coming, he turned around and left."

I let out my breath and slumped back on the couch in disappointment.

"I didn't tell any of this to the inspector; he wasn't interested in what I had to say. He just wanted to go through Flora's room."

"Do you know if he found anything?"

"No, like I said, that inspector pretty much ignored me, and those policemen made a dusty mess of the room, which I had to clean up. I did ask them what to do with Flora's things, and the inspector said to put them in storage after he finished with them. So, that's what I did. I wondered if someone might claim them. But no one has even asked about Flora since but you ladies."

"Could we possibly take a look at Flora's room, Mrs. Dowd?" I asked. "We don't want to be a bother, but…."

"But my Grandmother thinks Flora might have kept some estate paperwork and asked me if I could inquire after it," Binky stated with veracity.

"Well, you could look through her things I packed away in the attic, but her room's been let."

"Oh," Binky and I said in unison and looked at each other. "That would be very kind of you, Mrs. Dowd," I said.

Mrs. Dowd led us up two flights of creaky stairs and down a dim hallway. At its end, she stopped and reached into the pocket of her apron for a small bunch of keys. The landlady painstakingly read the label on one key after another. "Ah, here it is," she said, holding a key up in triumph. She bent over to unlock the door, but the knob turned freely and swung open wide. "That's funny," Mrs. Dowd said as she stepped into the room. "I always keep this door locked." She cautiously crossed to the center of the little storeroom, where an oil lantern hung suspended. She lit the lamp and crossed to the windows to pull up the shades. "Here we are now; Flora's things are over in this corner."

Mrs. Dowd guided us over to the corner behind the open door. There was a stack of new cartons. Every box lay open; the items ripped to shreds; clothes, books, shoes, everything. Not one thing remained undisturbed. The three of us stood in shocked silence. Mrs. Dowd began to tremble. Binky and I steadied her, helped her into the hallway, and sat her down on the top step. "Mrs. Dowd, I'm just going to loosen the top of your blouse so you can breathe easier, and then I want you to get your head below your heart by bending over and putting your head between your knees. This will allow more oxygen to reach your brain and ease the dizziness," Binky said in her VAD voice.

I ran downstairs to get Mrs. Dowd a glass of water. After a few wrong turns, I found the kitchen and dashed to the cupboard by the sink, where I found a small glass. I pumped the hand pump a few times, filled the glass with cold, free-flowing water, and then dampened a small tea towel. I turned to rush upstairs when I noticed the back door was open. I had a clear view of the porch and the coats that hung on pegs. Among them was a heavy topcoat. On the arm of the coat was a white band with a Red Cross.

I rushed upstairs. Mrs. Dowd still looked pale, but Binky had draped a warm blanket around her, which seemed to have stopped the shaking. I sat beside her on the step and put my arm around the landlady as she took small sips of water and then placed the dampened, folded tea towel at the back of her neck.

"How silly of me," Mrs. Dowd said with a shaky laugh. "I'm feeling better now; it was just such a shock to think someone was upstairs destroying Flora's belongings. Who would do such a thing?"

Neither Binky nor I wanted to state the obvious, so we ignored the question.

"Do you feel well enough to go downstairs?" Binky asked. "Let Alberta help you, and I'll lock up the storeroom."

Mrs. Dowd leaned heavily on me as she stood up and handed Binky the key ring. "Thank you," she said, and then without looking back, she grabbed my arm, and we descended slowly, one step at a time.

I got Mrs. Dowd down the stairs and had her lie on the couch with her feet elevated.

"Miss Holdaway, I'm fine, really I…."

"Now, Mrs. Dowd, lie there still until Binky gets here. She'll be just a minute; she was turning off the lights as we came down."

Binky entered the room and set the key ring on the tea table in front of the couch, then perched next to Mrs. Dowd. She took the woman's pulse, counting off the seconds on the mantel clock. Binky raised her eyes to her patient's face and smiled, "You'll do."

"I'm feeling much better. Please don't fuss," Mrs. Dowd protested. "May I sit up now?" She looked at me with a question on her face.

I reached out my two hands and grasped hers to help her upright. She sat still for a moment. "No dizziness; I feel fine now, right as rain, so silly of me. I've never done such a thing before."

"It was pretty shocking. You should notify the inspector, I suppose; he will probably want to collect those things."

Mrs. Dowd shook her head. "Oh dear, I hoped I'd seen the last of that man, but I suppose you're right. And I'll rest easier with that stuff out of this house." Mrs. Dowd started tearing up a bit, so I fussed with the tea things and poured her a fresh cup. We sat there drinking our tea for a few minutes when we heard footsteps coming up the front walk. Mrs. Dowd gasped and put her hand to her heart. Binky and I froze. There came a rattling at the front door and a slam.

"Mrs. Dowd!" bellowed a loud masculine voice, "you who."

"Professor Billingsley," exclaimed the landlady as she jumped up and crossed the room.

The man looked down with astonishment at the woman clinging to his chest and weeping. He looked up at Binky and me. "What on earth is going on?"

We explained everything to the poor bemused Professor, Mrs. Dowd's new lodger. The gentleman took Mrs. Dowd in hand and calmed her down. As the pair sat on the couch, Binky and I thanked the landlady and took our leave. "You stay right where you are; Miss Penrose and I can let ourselves out." I grasped the woman's hand and gave it a quick pat, then dragged Binky out of the room. Once out of sight, I detoured the kitchen and onto the back porch. "Look at this," I whispered, lifting the sleeve of the dark wool overcoat.

"Flora's?" Binky said with a sharp intake of breath.

"It must be," I said.

Binky quickly threw the coat over her arm as we fled out the back door.

Sergeant Colin

I was ever so happy to leave Mrs. Dowd's. This time *I* hailed the taxi. As soon as we pulled away from the curb, Binky lifted my bag, put it on the seat between us, and opened the lid. In the dim light, I could just make out Flora's coat.

"Binky, that's got to be tampering with evidence."

"Well, the inspector's boys had the first crack, didn't they?" Binky whispered.

"I don't think the inspector will see it that way. And what are we going to do with it?"

"You are going to take it with you to Highdrift, give it a thorough going over, and then take it to some obscure closet in Penrose House where I can just happen to come across it if needs be."

I sucked in my breath in astonishment and then put a hand to my mouth to muffle my nervous laughter. I struggled to gain my composure. "You and your grandmother are two peas in a pod."

"Why thank you," said Binky with her nose in the air. We rode the rest of the way to St. Hugh's in silence.

The taxi began to slow down as we neared the church graveyard. I leaned forward and tapped on the glass partition. "Driver, stop here, please."

"Are you sure I shouldn't come with you?" Binky asked. "I don't like you wandering the streets alone during the blackout."

"I won't wander; I'm going straight to the vicarage and then to Mrs. Pewter's. She's not far."

Binky lifted my chin and stared at my face. "Mm… I don't know; I can't tell if you're lying to me."

"I'll be fine; besides, I just finished my Red Cross self-defense course."

"Alberta…"

I gave Binky a quick hug and grabbed my suitcase. "Thanks for everything. I'll let you know if anything comes up." I slid across the seat and stepped out of the cab. I stood on the curb waving until the cab disappeared around the corner. I took a deep breath and willed myself to take the shortcut through St. Hugh's graveyard. I'd gone this way hundreds, maybe thousands of times. But something about seeing Flora's possessions destroyed instilled a small knot of fear within me. I took a firmer grip on my suitcase and slipped through the stone pillars that guarded the cemetery.

Actually, in the bright sunshine, this was a beautiful spot. I came here as a child and read by the hour, sitting in an old oak tree behind the Farringtons' Gothic Revival mausoleum. However, in the somber blackness of this spring night, with a slight breeze making the leaves flutter like a million bat wings, I wanted to run. I forced myself to stand still; I strained my eyes to make out familiar landmarks and tried to calm my pounding heart. I set out along the worn pavement listening carefully to each footfall. Other than a dog barking in the distance, I neither saw nor heard another living thing; until I reached the halfway point.

In the center of the graveyard was a massive marble cenotaph depicting St. Hugh ministering to the lepers. As soon as I walked behind this imposing edifice, my footsteps bombarded me in a violent echo. To calm my nerves, I thought of an old Irish prayer Mrs. Pewter taught me. It made me smile to think of it and her. I took a big breath and was about to recite it when I heard the ring of footsteps behind me. I stood statue-still, refusing to panic. I waited; silence. Then I heard it again. I began my prayer at the top of my lungs:

May those who love us, love us;
   And for those who don't love us,
   May God turn their hearts;
   And if He does not turn their hearts,
   May He turn their ankles,
   So we will know them by their limping.

The word "limping" echoed throughout the cemetery. I reached the edge of the cenotaph, stepped quickly to my left, and stopped, shielded by the massive monument. The footsteps behind me kept coming. I got a good grip on my suitcase; I twisted the case over to the left side of my body to put the maximum amount of force into my swing. Then I waited in strained silence. Footfalls came closer, closer, then stopped. A moment later, a dimmed torch flashed quickly, panned the immediate area, and flicked off again. My follower stood still. After a minute, the footsteps started again. Now I knew he was close. I watched at the edge of the building, waiting to see a dark form appear. The footsteps scraped closer and closer. I almost screamed as I tensed my muscles and raised the suitcase, ready to swing.

A solid form came into view, and my arms propelled the suitcase with all the force I could muster. I heard a grunt of pain. A body fell, and something metallic hit and skittered on the paved path. Suddenly a torch flicked on and spun like a child's top, throwing grisly shapes around the graveyard. I stood in shock as the world reeled. When the light finally stopped its crazy arc, it shined directly onto my pursuer. He wore a blue uniform with brass buttons. His helmet had flown off and was lying beside him; its police badge glowed gold. I got down on my hands and knees to peer closely at the policeman's face. His eyes opened and looked directly into mine. He struggled to speak, but the breath I had knocked out of him was yet to return. I reached out my hand and placed it on the man's shoulder, "What can I do for you? I'm so sorry, I thought... I don't know what." I sat back on my heels and saw the officer's face turn from pale to beet red. "I'm Alberta Holdaway. I used to live on the other side of St. Hugh's at the Vicarage. I was going there when I heard your footsteps."

The officer's breathing was ragged; his face contorted as he struggled to speak, "Bloody hell, you broke my rib! What did you hit me with a suitcase full of bricks?"

"Well, I will admit to a suitcase," I said as I stood up, "but not the bricks, and I do not appreciate your attitude. You could have hailed me and told me who you were, and I would not have hit you!"

I stooped to pick up the policeman's torch and switched it off.

"Blackout, you know, officer. You could be arrested." I grabbed my suitcase and handed him his light.

The officer struggled upright, gripping his left side. He swayed slightly, so I dropped my poor battered case on the ground, ran over, and put my arm around him.

"What do we do now? Maybe we should see if Mrs. Goolsby has any first aid supplies. I can wrap that rib for you."

"I'm okay; I just need to sit down and catch my breath. Maybe take an aspirin powder," the officer said. He leaned on me as we struggled up the walk. Then, as we reached the Vicarage steps, I shook off my arm and grabbed the railing. He pulled himself up, gingerly sat on the bench beside the front door, leaned back, and closed his eyes.

I forgot and almost walked straight into the Vicarage but stopped short and gave a loud knock. Feet shuffled down the hallway, then a voice grumbled, "All right, all right, I'm coming." The door opened a mere smidgen, "Who's there?"

"It's just me, Alberta, Mrs. Goolsby. Please, may I come in?" A little imp inside me made me add, "I have a bobbie with me." That did it. The door opened wide.

"What do you mean, the police?" she said as she thrust her face in mine. "What do we need with police? Come on in, my dear," she said, putting her arm around me in a motherly fashion. I stepped inside and waited, resisting Mrs. Goolsby's coercion. The officer's heavy tread sounded behind me. I turned and got my first real look at him in the light of the Vicarage hallway. He smiled, and I made the quick medical assessment that I had never seen a healthier specimen. I narrowed my eyes and gave him what I hoped was a suspicious and dirty look.

"I am Sergeant Colin, Mam," he said to Mrs. Goolsby.

Mrs. Goolsby paled, staggered back, and gripped the doorway

to keep her balance. Her reaction astonished me. I was relieved to see Ian Featherstone, the new Vicar, coming down the hall from the study. "Could I speak with you in private, Reverend Featherstone?" I asked.

The kindly old gentleman stepped aside and gestured for me to precede him to the study. I passed by him, and he turned to address the sergeant, "I'll be with you as soon as I can."

"I err…" the Sergeant looked at me.

I spoke up. "Mrs. Goolsby, poor Sergeant Colin has met with an accident and needs his ribs attended to. I know you helped with the Red Cross first aid course we held this spring. Maybe you could take a look." Mrs. Goolsby's eyes opened wide.

Revered Featherstone, and I entered the study. As the vicar closed the door, he whispered to me, "Poor man."

"Vicar Featherstone," I said, trying to keep my face straight.

"I know Alberta, but that woman is a trial and that son of hers. They turn everyone away. She's rude, and he's decidedly odd. It was a sad day for this parish when you and your father left, and Mrs. Pewter went to live with her sister."

"Father always said Mrs. Pewter did most of the ministering in the kitchen with her teapot."

Vicar Featherstone nodded. "Goolsby's gone, you know."

"No, I didn't know," I said.

"Martin enlisted, or so Mrs. Goolsby tells me."

"Oh, I got the impression he'd tried before, and they wouldn't take him."

"Well, they're scraping the bottom of the barrel these days; take anyone." Vicar Featherstone sighed and sat in his hard swivel chair. He looked up at me. "How can I help?"

"You heard Father has been arrested?"

The Vicar nodded his head, "Ridiculous, absolutely!"

"It's funny; everyone says that, but there he sits in jail."

"Inspector Blodgett was here."

"I'm not surprised. Blodgett thinks all clergymen are shirkers, I gather."

"Oh? He didn't strike me that way. Seemed very concerned for your father and you."

"Me, why would he be concerned about me?"

"Blodgett asked about your connection with Miss Hicks and if I knew anyone with a grudge against you and your father. Didn't like that attack you suffered at Paddington."

"Attack? But Blodgett said it was just an accident."

"Was it?" Vicar Featherstone said. "Was it indeed."

As I sat digesting this new idea, the Vicar reached into the desk and brought out his Meerschaum. He lifted it and looked at me with his bushy eyebrows raised. I nodded, saying nothing. I watched his arthritic old fingers perform the ritual of lighting his pipe.

He puffed a few times, then leaned back. The cherry-like smoke scented the room. "If someone wanted your father to be alone on the train, with no alibi, you were in the way."

"So you think whoever killed Flora knocked me down to prevent my getting on the train?"

"Could be. Or there might have been an accomplice; I don't know. But I do know the inspector is keeping an eye on you."

"An eye on me! For my protection? He probably thinks I am involved directly in Flora's death. I suppose I could have gone to the baggage car and bonked her on the head."

"Well, for whatever reason, Sergeant Colin is keeping a close watch."

My Bodyguard

Sergeant Colin and I trudged up the rickety third-floor staircase that led to the attic. I don't think I have ever met a man that whined and complained so much. He kept up a constant flow, mostly complaining about Mrs. Goolsby's treatment. I was glad I was leading the way so he couldn't see the smile on my face.

I reached the top of the staircase and stepped to the side so the sergeant could shine the oil lamp on the door ahead of me. "We never locked the attic when Father and I lived here," I said. "It seems silly. No one can make it past Mrs. Goolsby."

"Inspector Blodgett's orders," Sergeant Colin said.

"Like his order for you to follow me?"

"Vicar Featherstone wasn't supposed to tell you that."

"I've known Vicar Featherstone all my life. He thought it would make me feel better to know Inspector Blodgett was concerned. And, to be honest, Sergeant Colin, whether Inspector Blodgett is concerned about me or suspicious of me,

I do feel much safer with you around. Now that I know you are around, that is."

"Well, that's good because my orders are to stick with you as long as you're in London." Sergeant Colin unlocked the attic door and stepped in. I started to follow him, and he held out his hand and stopped me. The attic was dark and close. Each step sent dust swirling in the air. I sneezed as Sergeant Colin let go of me and pointed at the floor. He lowered the lamp; it highlighted a crisscross of lines over the wooden surface. "I was supposed to be the last person in here," he said, "but look at all those tracks in the dust. Things have been moved and dragged about the floor."

"I don't know why all of our things were moved up here in the first place. We stored all of our things in the guest room. When Father left it was to be a short stay to recuperate, not a permanent move."

"Maybe we should ask Mrs. Goolsby."

"Of course, she'd know, but can I look through these things first? I have to get some books for Father and my camera and arrange to have everything else sent to Highdrift."

"You're not returning here then?"

"No, Father and I will not be back."

From out in the hall came a slight creak of a floorboard, Sergeant Colin and I paused to listen. Then a stealthy tiptoeing approached the attic door.

Mrs. Goolsby poked her head in, "Vicar Featherstone sent me up here to help."

"Mrs. Goolsby," I asked, "why were our things moved up here and who was in this room last?"

"The guest room was needed by the Vicar. I had Martin haul your things up." Mrs. Goolsby nodded in Sergeant Colin's direction, "This Sergeant here was the last one in this room. He locked the door behind him."

"But Mrs. Goolsby, someone has been up here going through and rearranging our things. You must have heard something."

Mrs. Goolsby stepped towards me and put her hands on her hips, "Are you calling me a liar?"

I wanted to say yes, but instead, I ignored her, knelt next to the box marked "photo," and began looking for my camera. "That's impossible, I know my camera was in here. I put it in this little wooden box wrapped in paper." I looked up at Mrs. Goolsby.

"I suppose you'll blame that on me too," she said, then stomped from the room.

"Phew, poor Vicar Featherstone," was all Sergeant Colin had to say as he listened to Mrs. Goolsby bang and clang her way downstairs.

I bent down again to sort through the rest of the box. "All my photos are here but look at these. These aren't mine. They are similar to the photo Saben Best showed me of Flora Hicks." I looked up at Sergeant Colin; tears filled my eyes.

"Here, now; none of that. Let me see." He looked at the photos I held out to him, then dropped on his knee beside me on the dusty floor and turned the small carton over. "Now look here, I made my initial on the bottom of every box that was searched."

I looked where Sergeant Colin pointed and saw the small *CC*. "So that means?"

"That means those pictures were added to that box after these cartons were searched. The inspector looked through every photo and letter looking for evidence. He knew what Flora Hicks looked like. He would not have missed those. I had better get in touch with the inspector to see what he wants me to do about this. Let me put these pictures back, we better leave everything as it is. I'll see that all this gets sent on to Lanmorech when I get the nod from the inspector."

I stood and brushed the dust from my skirt. "Do you have any idea how long that will take? I'll be at Mrs. Pewter's tomorrow."

"I can't say, I don't imagine the inspector will be able to spend too much time on this, the department is stretched pretty thin."

After saying farewell to Vicar Featherston, Sergeant Colin and I made our departure. He insisted on carrying my suitcase across Froggatt's Park to the slightly run-down middle-class neighborhood of Chumston. We walked in silence until we reached Number 27.

"Our old housekeeper, Mrs. Pewter, lives here with her sister," I informed him as we approached the residence.

"I know," Sergeant Colin said, "I spoke to Mrs. Pewter briefly at the Vicarage right after the incident. She said she would be moving here."

I opened my mouth to question him and then decided it was better to keep silent. I stepped onto the front porch and noticed the change in Number 27 right away. It looked scrupulously neat and tidy even in the dim moonlight. I turned the brass knob in the middle of the front door labeled 'bell.' I heard a low ding, the door opened. Mrs. Pewter's sister, Nancy, instantly smothered me against her lilac-scented bosom and held me in a viselike grip, "Alberta, my dear, so nice, so nice. And who is this handsome man you have in tow?" Nancy extended her free hand to Sergeant Colin. I saw his eyes widen in pain as he felt the strength of Nancy's handclasp.

"This is Sergeant Colin, he is, what are you exactly, Sergeant?"

"I am Miss Holdaway's bodyguard."

"Bodyguard who needs a bodyguard?" said Mrs. Pewter as

she came from the kitchen, wiping her hands on her gleaming white apron.

"No one, the sergeant is just being facetious," I said as I hugged Mrs. Pewter.

"And do we have a first name?" Nancy asked the police officer as she put her trunk-like arm around Sergeant Colin's broad shoulders.

"Cathcart."

Nancy stopped dead, mouth wide open. For the first time since we entered the house, there was utter silence. What do you say to a name like Cathcart? "Oh, umm, yes, now let's see," twittered Nancy, "let's go into the sitting room and relax."

Nancy and the sergeant walked ahead, and Mrs. Pewter leaned nearer to me, "How is your father doing?" she whispered.

"Fine, better than I hoped, actually; some very nice people in Lanmorech are trying their hardest to find out what really happened. We've both been given a lot of support."

"Thank God, I have been so worried about you both," said Mrs. Pewter.

"S'cuse me ladies I need to get back to headquarters. Just wanted to see Alberta, umm, Miss Holdaway, home," said Sergeant Colin. "And no need to see me out. You ladies remain just as you are." Then the Sergeant turned to me, "Now you behave yourself and stay here, I'll pick you up tomorrow and take you to the train. Good night." Before I could think of a suitable rejoinder, he was gone.

"Well," said Mrs. Pewter, "what was all that about?"

"I should be hopeful, I guess, that Inspector Blodgett is keeping an open mind about Flora Hick's death," I sank down, tense and exhausted, on the sofa.

A warm hand covered my own. "Tell me what's happened,"

Mrs. Pewter said.

"I found out coming up on the train that someone saw Father actually leaving the Postal car. Some stewardess or other, I spoke to her myself."

"I won't believe that, it's not possible, so there must be another explanation. Nan, what do you think?"

"Did the witness say she saw your father's face or just some man from the back she thought looked like the Vicar?" Nancy asked.

"What she said exactly was that she saw, 'a clergyman leave the Postal car, she saw his white clerical collar.'"

"Hmm, that does narrow the field a bit."

"Anyone could turn their shirt backward and look like a cleric. That means almost nothing," said Mrs. Pewter.

"Still, it looks bad," I said.

"Mmm, well let's forget it for tonight. You look like you need a cup of Nan's Valerian tea and a good lie-in. We'll tackle this fresh in the morning."

There's nothing more relaxing than being pampered and ordered about. I simply did as I was told and slept.

The next morning I sat in the tiny breakfast nook in Nancy Nash's kitchen. Mrs. Pewter fixed a plate of fried potatoes, bacon, and eggs. I ate my first full meal for days. As I ate my last bite of toast, covered with Mrs. Pewter's homemade orange marmalade, I said, "Are you sure you can spare the bread and eggs."

"It's a little late to bemoan your gluttony now you've cleaned your plate," said Mrs. Pewter, with a smile.

"I know, that's why I waited until I finished every crumb. I was starved."

"Who's a glutton?" said a familiar voice from the hallway.

Binky Penrose walked into the kitchen and gave Mrs. Pewter a big hug.

"Me, who else," I laughed. "What in the world are you doing here?"

"I need you to do me a big favor."

"Oh, oh, that doesn't sound too good."

"I should restate that," Binky said as she sat across from me in the breakfast nook. "I need you to do Granny a favor. Friends of hers have a granddaughter they want to send down to Cornwall for the duration of the war. The child can't leave until late this evening. I know the *Night Riviera* probably isn't your first choice of transportation home, but everyone would be very grateful if you could escort her down."

"Yes, of course, I'll help. How do I collect her?"

"You don't have to, I'll bring her to Paddington tonight and see you aboard." Binky leaned toward me and lowered her voice. "Alberta, did you look at the coat?" Binky silently mouthed, "Flora's coat."

I shook my head. Binky rolled her eyes. She stood and put her hands on her hips. "Where is it?"

"Upstairs in the guestroom, in my case," I scooted across the bench seat.

Binky grabbed my arm and led me upstairs. "Where is your room?"

"End of the hall, right side."

Binky opened the door and immediately zeroed in on the battered suitcase sitting next to the dresser. She flung it on the neatly made bed. "Here Alberta, you open it."

I touched the two brass latches on either side of the case; they sprung open with a ping. I flipped open the lid. Underneath my clothes lay the dead girl's black wool coat. I reached my hand

133

forward then stopped.

"Here," Binky said, "let me." Piece by piece, Binky emptied my things onto the bed. She lifted out the coat, gently laid it over the case, and then slid her hand into a pocket. She shivered a little. "This is a bit creepy," Binky said as she looked at me.

"Find anything?"

"Not in this one." Binky checked the other side, then the inner breast pocket. She straightened up, "Shucks, I thought we'd surely find something."

I let out a whoosh of breath. "Let's get this packed back up."

"Relax," said Binky, "no one will know this isn't yours."

"Why would I pack a wool coat in June?"

"Well, maybe you picked it up at the Vicarage to take back to Highdrift."

"The coat still makes me nervous, please pack it away."

Binky put everything neatly back in the suitcase. "That's that, I had better skedaddle. Meet you at Paddington. I'll have Piper there at 11:00." Binky opened her purse and pulled out a train ticket. "Here, this is yours. See you tonight and thanks a million." Binky gave me a quick peck on the cheek and left the room.

That's about as old as I felt, a million. I plopped on the bed next to the suitcase and stared at the train ticket clutched in my hand.

Piper at Paddington

Before the war, Paddington Station at 11:00 p.m. was a mellow reflection of its daytime self. But now, quite a queue of uniformed servicemen gathered around the British Red Cross Rest Station. As I drew closer to the long service counter, heaped high with coffee cups, Binky Penrose's distinctive laugh rang out, and then a chorus of servicemen joined in.

"May I give you a small tip, little lassie?" One of the soldiers said as he accepted a doughnut and a cup of coffee from a little girl with long braids.

"Oh no, Sir, the Red Cross does not allow us to accept gratuities." The crowd chuckled and guffawed, and the soldiers continued chatting to Binky and her diminutive charge while they enjoyed this brief respite from the realities of war. I lifted my hand. Binky spotted me. She went up to the counter, lifted the trap door, stepped from beneath it, and then closed the door behind her.

"Bertie, come meet your charge." She grabbed my wrist and

dragged me forward into the middle of a sea of uniforms. My skin grew warm with embarrassment. I tried to halt my forward momentum and bumped into the back of a very large man in a dark blue uniform who looked familiar.

"Whoa," the man's coffee cup flew from his hands and flipped up in the air. The cup spewed swirls of hot coffee as the officer in blue spun around in an instinctive pirouette and, in a surprising show of manual dexterity, caught the tumbling coffee cup in one hand while still gripping the saucer in the other. The crowd milling about the Rest Station erupted in applause. When he held the cup up triumphantly and turned, I recognized him.

"Excuse me, Sergeant Colin," I said, my face redder than ever.

"I should have known. Can't you just shake hands or something? Every time I come upon you unexpectedly, I get hurt and totally messed about," the sergeant said.

Binky stepped forward and held out her hand to the damp policeman. "It was my fault, really …."

"Lawanda Penrose, this is Sergeant Colin," I said.

"Ohh, so this is the man you were complaining about. Nice to meet you, Sergeant." The handsome officer proffered the empty coffee cup and saucer. Binky looked at her outstretched palm, then threw back her head and laughed. She slipped her arm through the Sergeant's and guided him to the bar. "You stand right here, Sergeant Colin, and we'll get you set to rights."

"Oh no, I'll just go on over there to the men's room and wash up, thanks." Sergeant Colin gently removed Binky's hand from the crook of his arm and walked across the shiny station floor, his dampened shoes squeaking all the way.

Just then, there was a tug on my skirt. I looked down into the earnest spectacles of the little girl in braids. The child held a mop aloft, which was twice her size. "Excuse me," said the little girl, "I am supposed to clean up this spill before someone slips and injures themselves. If you could step aside, please?"

"Oh, surely."

Binky and I stood aside to watch the little girl, tongue showing at the corner of her mouth, struggle with the oversized floor mop. The girl stopped, dissatisfied with the results of her cleaning, and looked up at me. "I seem to be making matters worse."

"Here, let me go wring that out, and we'll try again." I went around the back corner of the Rest Station and returned with an extra mop and some rags. The child and I mopped and dried the floor until just a trace of dampness remained.

As we surveyed our handiwork, we heard sticky footsteps approach. "Are you ladies ready to get aboard the train?" said Sergeant Colin.

"We are, but you needn't see me off, Sergeant," I said.

"I am not seeing you off," said Sergeant Colin, "I'm accompanying you."

"Oh, now, really, that's not necessary," I sputtered.

The police officer put his hand up to silence my protests, "Inspector's orders."

I sighed, turned on my heel, gripped the little girl's hand, and led her to the front of the Rest Station. I spotted Binky and walked towards her. "Great job, you two," Binky said. "Here, Piper, let's get your suitcase from behind the bar, and then we'll get you situated on the train, shall we?"

"I think this man is taking us, Miss Binky."

"Oh?" Binky said as she returned with the case. "Here then, Sergeant, you may as well play porter."

"I've had worse jobs, Miss Penrose." The sergeant held one

hand out for the suitcase and the other to Piper. The little girl eagerly clutched it and skipped along beside him. Piper chattered like a magpie, and the sergeant listened intently to every word.

Binky and I watched the sergeant squat down and answer the little girl's question with serious intensity, "What a nice man," Binky said.

"Humph, he is Inspector Blodgett's stooge," I said.

"And why should Inspector Blodgett have an officer see you back to Lanmorech?"

"Well, Sergeant Colin says for my protection, but I think they are looking for more evidence against Father."

"You make sure to be careful with that VAD overcoat then," whispered Binky. "We don't want the inspector getting wind of that. Take it to Penrose as soon as you can. It wouldn't do for the coat to be found at Highdrift." Binky thrust her hand into her pocket. "Oh, I almost forgot, I have a letter for you from Red Cross Headquarters. I kind of know what's in it, but you are to read it in private and mention the letter to no one."

"Why all the mystery?" I asked.

"I hate to say this, not wanting to sound like Inspector Blodgett, but for your own protection."

Saben's Daughter

As I entered the compartment, Sergeant Colin and Piper were already seated and chatting away like old friends. I stowed away my battered suitcase and hung my Burberry trench coat in the tiny closet. Then slipped off my hat and took a quick peek in the mirror. I patted my hair and gave my wilted white shirtwaist a tweak and navy linen skirt a light brush. I caught Sergeant Colin's glance in the mirror and turned around just as the sergeant stood. "I'm in the next compartment; tap on the door if you need anything. Remember to lock up." He turned to Piper, bowed, and held out his hand, "Good night Miss Piper; sleep well."

"Good night Sergeant Colin; thank you for carrying my suitcase," Piper's eyes twinkled behind her wire rims as she held out her hand. The sergeant smiled and nodded, then slipped through the compartment door into the corridor.

"Phew, you must be exhausted; I know I am. Here I'll ring for the porter to make up the beds." I reached over and pressed the small white button set into the oak paneling. There was a light tap at the cabin door in a few minutes.

The steward popped his head in, "May I make up your berths, Miss?"

"Yes, please." I held out my hand to Piper. "Should we get out of the way? We could go get a quick midnight snack." Piper bounced up off the banquette and took my hand. There came a great groan and whoosh as the train's engine started gathering momentum. After one final burst of steam, the train began its nightly departure from Paddington Station.

"Oh, Miss, we're moving," Piper said as she dropped my hand and pressed her face to the window.

I smiled at Piper's excitement and joined her at the window to watch the train leisurely pass by the First Class lounge with GWR in huge gilt letters. Next came the tea shop, the booksellers, and finally, the Red Cross Rest Station, still thronged by servicemen. Piper smiled and gave a frantic wave, and some of the men waved back. What a nice child, I thought, as we exited the train station and sped into the darkened city. "Come, Piper, let's get out of the steward's way." We left the compartment. The little girl walked before me down the dimly lit train corridor. Suddenly she stopped dead, closed her eyes, and held her arms outstretched. I stopped, too, and watched. *What in the world was she doing?* I was about to say something when she let out a whoosh of breath and resumed her forward progress, virtually skipping down the corridor.

We crossed into the next car. Piper asked, "Do we go much further?"

"Just through one more car." Piper grabbed my hand, and we rushed ahead. We went through another accordion-like connection and came to a door with an oval window etched with frosted filigree. I opened the door and ushered Piper in.

140

"Oh, lovely," Piper said as we crossed a velvety plush carpet to a booth of highly polished wood and blue and gold fabric. Each table had its own small leaded glass lamp. Deep blue velvet curtains framed wide picture windows that reflected the car's interior like ebony mirrors. I watched Piper's reflection as she slipped into a high-backed tapestry-covered booth. She reached into the pocket of her green jumper to pull out a small leather notebook and pencil and then scribbled like mad.

I sat down opposite. "I'll just order us something then." Piper was quite absorbed and did not answer. I waited a moment and then looked around for a waiter. The car was empty, but voices came from the adjacent Lounge Car. "I'll be right back," I said. Piper looked at me and smiled, then bent her head again and continued writing. I scooted from the booth, walked down the aisle, and entered the Lounge. Dim lighting, and small groupings of club chairs, made the space warm and intimate. Except for the train's motion and sound, this could be a tiny London club. A few passengers sat here and there, deep in conversation. No one took note of me as I walked up to the bar. "Excuse me," I said to the barkeep, "may I order a glass of Horlicks, some biscuits, and a pot of tea, please."

The barman lay his white polishing towel down on the bar, "Yes, Miss, but I'm sorry to say we are short on sugar."

"That's fine; I've gotten used to that. My companion is a young girl, and we are seated in the Restaurant car."

"You are welcome to sit in here if it would please you to do so."

"Wonderful, we'll be right along." I turned from the bar and noticed a woman passenger sitting in the corner, alone, staring out into the passing night. Her face was in profile. The polished glass of the train's window acted as a dark mirror; it was Miss

Briggs. I hesitated but then rushed past without saying anything. I would say hello after I collected Piper.

I went back to the Restaurant Car. Piper set her notebook aside and positively beamed at me. "This is so exciting. I can't imagine how fast we must be going."

"We get to have our tea in the Lounge; you can ask the barman. I bet he knows the train's speed." I waited for Piper to bounce across the booth seat and join me in the aisle.

Piper clutched her leather-bound notebook and gave me an owlish glance. "Why is this train called the *Night Riviera?*"

"Oh ah, well, I believe that Cornwall, our destination, is known as the English Riviera. Riviera means "shore" in Italian," I said as I ushered Piper down the corridor. "The real Riviera is on the Mediterranean Sea and goes from France to Italy. However, Cornwall has similarities in climate and terrain. There are palm trees and lovely beaches, and it is a place for families to vacation."

We entered the Lounge. I glanced to my left; the table was empty; Miss Briggs was gone. I ushered Piper before me and picked a table. As Piper sat and made herself comfortable, I finished my lecture. "The reason for the term 'Night' is because it is an overnight sleeper train. Now, when I came up to London a few days ago, I took the *Cornish Riviera Express*, which runs in the morning with just a few stops."

A slight furrow appeared on Piper's brow, and one eyebrow tweaked up above the metal frame of her spectacles, "Hmm," she said.

"Here we are, ladies, tea and Horlicks," said the waiter with a smile. He held a gleaming silver tray with one hand and deftly set our libation before us.

Piper took a dainty sip of her malted milk and patted her

mouth with the linen napkin."Grandmother Reed never allows me a late-night snack. She tells me it will foster nightmares."

"Foster nightmares? Oh dear, I hope not," I said.

"Grandmother Reed is always right. At least that's what Grandfather says."

"Your grandmother sounds like a formidable woman."

"She is. My other grandmother is a Gypsy."

"A Gypsy... is Morvah Best your grandmother?"

Piper took another sip of Horlick's and then nodded. She sat up straight, lifted her chin, and said with pride, "Yes, and Constable Saben Best is my father; he's a war hero and a policeman."

I sat in silence, stunned. Now that I thought about it, I had never discussed anything personal with either Saben or Morvah. I smiled at Piper, "I have met them. They seem very nice."

Piper had her head down, and her notebook open on the table. She scribbled furiously. "They are both wonderful," she said without lifting her gaze from the creamy-colored pages. "I am excited to live in Lanmorech. I have never been." Piper paused in her writing and lifted her head, "May I ask the barman how fast we are going?" I nodded my head. Piper jumped up, gathered her notebook and pencil, and carefully made her way down the aisle to the end of the car.

I sat and watched her. I noticed tiny bits of Saben Best in her movements, features, and gestures. Piper was fair, whereas Saben was dark, but there was a multitude of similarities. I wondered about her mother. Where was she?

Saben's daughter was back in a flash. "The *Night Riviera* can go up to 70 miles an hour. We aren't going that fast, though." The little girl paused and read from her notebook. "War regulations limit the speed to forty to save on fuel. Isn't that amazing? And look at the tea in your cup; it barely jiggles. This is a lovely way to travel." Piper sat down with a sigh.

"Yes, it's a lovely way. Now, finish your milk, and let's get back to our cabin."

Intruder on a Train

Piper and I stepped into our compact little cabin. The steward had turned on the small reading lamps at the head of each bunk, and they bathed the room in a warm, golden glow. Bright, white pillows and sheets peaked out from beneath plush blue coverlets. I switched on the small table lamp as Piper rushed around me.

"May I sleep on the top bunk, Miss Holdaway, please?"

"Are you sure? What if your Grandmother Reed is right?"

"She isn't, not this time, and look; there is a small net along the outside. I won't fall off."

"Oh, all right, you get your nightie on and wash up in that little sink over there and off to bed; it's late." Piper nodded, and without another word, she opened her case and plucked out her night things. As the little girl bustled about, I rummaged in the closet for my coat. I reached into the pocket for the letter Binky handed me at the station. I felt in one pocket then the other, no letter. I paused; I knew I had stuffed it in my coat. I lifted the trench coat off the hanger and draped it on my bunk. I rechecked the pockets. This time I noticed a long slice in the bottom seam. I slid my hand inside the lining and felt the edge of the envelope. I pulled it out. "Miss Alberta Holdaway, VAD," the bright white business envelope read. I recognized Mrs. Brodie's elegant copperplate.

"I'm done, Miss Holdaway. Can you help me up?"

"Oh, ah… yes, just one moment." I lay the letter on the gleaming wood table and turned. Piper stood before me in a long white nightgown, her pink toes peeking from under its ruffled hem. "Here we are; up you go."

Piper clambered onto the upper bunk, light as a feather and agile as a monkey. She crawled on hands and knees to its head and slid beneath the crisp white sheets. "Oh, I forgot to take off my glasses." Piper handed me her wire-rimmed spectacles. I carefully folded them and set them on the table beside my letter. Then tucked the soft blankets around my diminutive charge.

"Sleep tight, dear; say your prayers." I switched off the bunk light. Piper folded her hands and closed her eyes. I picked up my letter and sat on the lower berth. I slid my thumb under the corner of the envelope flap, tore it open, and moved, so the Tiffany-shaded lamp illuminated the flowing script. Mrs. Brodie requested that I inventory the pearl drive proceeds and arrange for their secure transport to London. She went on to caution me to speak about this as little as possible. My heart pounded; I leaned back and closed my eyes, suddenly very tired. I would help the Red Cross in any way I could, but the thought of those pearls and their connection with Flora's murder scared me.

By the time I readied myself for bed, I had formulated a plan. Since Scotland Yard had provided me with a "bodyguard," I would put him to good use. I would inventory the Red Cross pearls as soon as possible and send them to London with Sergeant Colin. That would get rid of two significant problems at the same time. I snapped off my light, snuggled down, and forced myself to relax in the darkness. I fell into a fitful sleep. I tossed and turned, plumped my pillow, and got up for a sip of water. I laid back down and finally slept hard.

So hard that it wasn't until I heard Piper's whisper that I awoke. "Alberta, Miss Holdaway." My eyes flew open, and I saw the shadow of Piper's head upside down with her braids dangling before me. I let out a stifled scream. I heard some muffled thuds, and then a ribbon of light filled the room as someone opened the cabin door and fled into the corridor.

A few moments later, there was pounding on the connecting door to Sergeant Colin's cabin. "Miss Holdaway, are you all right? Open the door!"

I got out of bed and groped around for my robe. "Just a moment, we are fine, just a moment." I unlocked the connecting door, and Sergeant Colin fell into the tiny, five-by-eight space. He regained his balance and took me by the shoulders. His eyes searched my face, illuminated by the light filtering from his compartment.

"I heard you scream."

"Piper just startled me. I didn't realize anyone was in here until they weren't." I slipped from the Sergeant's grasp and flicked on the overhead light.

He whistled, "What a mess."

What a mess, indeed. The contents of my suitcase were strewn all about the cabin. Out in plain sight was Flora Hicks's VAD overcoat. I snatched it up and stuffed it out of sight.

"Hey now, you shouldn't do that. We need to document and

147

report this break-in."

"No, Sergeant Colin, I'm sure someone just entered this cabin in error. Someone came in by mistake and picked up my case, thinking it was their own. The latch on that case is loose and gives way all the time." I pushed Sergeant Colin towards his room, through the door, and shut it in his face as politely as I could. Then leaned against it. Repeated knocks reverberated through my body as he banged on the door. I looked up at Piper, who sat on the edge of the upper train bunk, eyes wide in her pale face. The pounding ceased; I waited a minute and was just about to pick up the mess when Sergeant Colin bellowed, "Lock your door!"

I did as ordered, went over to my bunk, and began to tuck Piper back in bed. "Are you all right?"

"Yes, I guess so. I am glad Sergeant Colin is next door, though."

"You know what?" I said in a whisper, "I am too." I quickly picked up the clothes lying about, folded them, and stuffed them back in my suitcase. I made sure to conceal the VAD coat at the bottom. Then I slipped off my robe, returned to my bunk, and flicked off the light. I put my hands behind my head and tried to relax. But the question of why someone would break into my cabin and riffle my suitcase baffled me. I lied to Sergeant Colin about my case latch being faulty. What could an intruder be searching for? No one but Binky knew I had Flora's coat.

Home to Highdrift

I opened my eyes the next morning to the shimmer of water, or I should say its reflection, as it played upon our train compartment's ceiling. I glanced at my watch, which hung on a small brass hook, seven o'clock. The steward would bring breakfast soon. I threw back the covers and sat on the edge of my berth. To my delight, out the window, the majestic form of St. Michael's Mount rose, in solitude, from Mount's Bay. No matter how many times I see the sight, it astounds me.

I gazed upward to see if Piper was awake. She lay on her stomach, peering out of the train's window at the view, and began to recite:

"And whilst the dazzling sun-beams play
On the blue waters of the bay,
From this high cliff, where ravens soar,
I'll hearken to the billows roar,
Or hold dark converse with the sprite
That guards St. Michael's holy height."

"How lovely, aren't you clever," I said as I picked up Piper's glasses and handed them to her. She slid them on and made her way off the upper berth.

"When Grandma told me I was coming to Cornwall, I read all about King Arthur and the Knights of the Round Table. I read that Arthur battled with a local giant on St. Michael's Mount. Da said he would take me there; would you come too?"

"Oh, we'll see, now get dressed, breakfast…." Just as I uttered the word, there was a discrete tap at the door. "Come in."

"Good morning, ladies. I hope you slept well," the steward put a tray on the small table under the window. "Here is the breakfast you ordered. We will pull into Penzance Station soon, right on time." With that, he backed out of the compartment and shut the door. We could hear the food trolley bang along the corridor as he proceeded on his way.

Piper and I ate a light breakfast and were washed, dressed, and packed when the whistle blew. We collected our things as the train came to a halt. I lowered the window, reached outside, and undid the latch. I stepped onto the concourse and was about to turn for Piper when Sergeant Colin came up beside me and helped her down. The policeman took the overnight cases from my hand. The three of us strolled amongst the other passengers under the high curved iron and glass ceiling towards the black iron gates. We went through the barricade and headed into the enclosed waiting room. Piper spotted her father waiting near the door and immediately ran to him. Saben bent down and gathered his daughter into his arms. "Oh, Da," came Piper's muffled voice.

I didn't want to intrude, so I turned to Sergeant Colin. "Um…, do you need a lift to Lanmorech?"

"If I'm not mistaken, Inspector Blodgett has arranged for

Constable Best to give us a lift."

Saben and Piper came up behind us, "That's right; someone dropped me off, so I'll drive you in the estate car."

"All right, just let me make a few shipping arrangements, and I'll be right back." I made my way to the small queue before the luggage claim. In a few minutes, I presented my tickets through the grilled window. The elderly man behind the counter gave them to a youngish woman in railroad livery who disappeared into the back room full of cases and crates.

"You Miss Holdaway, are ya? Ta' Highdrift?" the elderly man said.

"Yes, I am."

"Well, I've got somethin' else here awaitin' ya.'" The old man turned and yelled over his shoulder, "Jennie, bring out the special delivery for Highdrift!"

"But I want to arrange to have my crates delivered home to Highdrift."

"Oh, now, Miss, this "Special" should maybe go along with ya' now, seein's you've got transportation, like."

Jennie appeared from around the back, pushing a baggage trolley. On the trolley sat a good-sized box with holes in it. I heard a familiar wheeze, then a low growl. "Peachy?" Sharp barks echoed through the terminal, and the wooden crate began to bump and rock. "Oh my gosh, Peachy, what on earth?"

Saben and Piper walked up to me; Saben handed me a note, "This was sent to your Father just after you left for London."

The note read, *Dear Vicar Holdaway and Alberta,*

I have taken your advice and moved in with my sister, Beulah, who resides in Sussex. As you know, my sister (says she) is allergic to dogs (I think it may just be Peachy she's allergic to), and Peachy mayn't come with me.

151

You so graciously offered to help me in any way when last we met, so I'm sending my darling to you for the duration. I'm sure she will give you no trouble.

With Sincerest Gratitude,

Mildred Crumpet

It was a case of laughing or crying. Therefore, I crumpled the letter and doubled over in laughter. From this position, I could see the elderly bulldog shiver in her holey doghouse. This cut my hilarity short. I reached to undo the latch on the large wooden box and set Peachy free of her prison. "Did she come with a lead or harness, perhaps?" I asked the female attendant.

"Oh, yes, Miss, I have a package right here." Jennie gave me a small carton containing all Peachy's worldly goods.

"Now, my girl, let's get you out of there." I opened the latch, but the old dog scooted to the back of the crate and sat down with a stubborn expression on her homely face. Piper stepped to my side and knelt; she reached her hand towards Peachy and crooned a string of baby talk, just as Mrs. Crumpet had done countless times. Peachy sniffed the proffered fingers and gave them a little lick. Then the pink and portly pooch leaped into Piper's outstretched arms. Both dog and little girl sprawled on the chilly pavement. Saben bent to pick up his daughter, and I clipped a lead on Peachy's collar.

The drive to Lanmorech went by speedily. I relaxed in the cramped backseat while Piper petted and chatted with the elderly bulldog. Saben drove, and Sergeant Colin filled him in on the break-ins. The first, in the attic at the Vicarage, and the second, in my train compartment. The sergeant did not believe my tale about the suitcase latch. Which proves I'm a terrible liar.

I attempted to listen to the conversation in the front seat, but the road noise made eavesdropping a hit-and-miss affair. It suddenly struck me how low an amateur must sink to be productive at detection. But I had no qualms about such subterfuge if it would bring my father home.

"Isn't that right, Miss Holdaway?" said Sergeant Colin.

"Pardon me?"

"Wasn't Mrs. Goolsby hostile and acting suspiciously."

"Well, yes, she was, but that's her normal demeanor. That's why we employed Mrs. Pewter and let Mrs. Goolsby go."

"So, Vicar Holdaway fired the Goolsby woman?" Saben asked me over his shoulder.

"That was years ago when my mother was alive. She let Mrs. Goolsby go."

"So, could the housekeeper have a grudge against your father?"

"Yes, she probably does, but not for that reason. Mrs. Goolsby hates Father because Martin went before a tribunal and lost his deferral from military service. Martin had a deferment because Mrs. Goolsby said he was her only child. But it turned out he is not Mrs. Goolsby's."

"So, how did your Father come into the case," asked Sergeant Colin.

"Well, Father was asked point-blank about Martin, and he knew Martin was the Goolsby's nephew, not their son. He had no choice but to tell the truth."

"Hmm…" said Saben, "Food for thought." Then he changed the subject. "Now, Piper, here we are; this is Lanmorech. Look over there; it's your Gran, come to greet you." Saben pulled up in front of the long gray wharf. Morvah Best sat on a wooden bench in the sunshine, waiting for her son and granddaughter. As soon as the automobile halted, I reached over dog and child

153

and opened the passenger door. Piper slid out, taking the fat bulldog with her.

"My darling," Morvah said as she held out her arms. Piper ran to her grandmother, dragging Peachy along. "And who is this?" Morvah asked.

"This is Miss Alberta's dog, Peachy."

Morvah gave me a questioning look over the top of her glasses. I shrugged my shoulders and lifted my hands, "Peachy is a refugee from London, sent by a parishioner and old friend of the family," I explained.

"She seems a bit overweight, Alberta. This visit will do the animal good, I think. A pet may do your father some good as well. He will need a companion after you return to London."

"Yes, I suppose so . . . ."

"Well, I'll leave Piper with you, Mother. Um . . . , Colin, can I drop you here?"

"Oh, sure, Best, I'll just hoof it to the Inn, thanks." The Sergeant grabbed his bag from the boot, "Goodbye, Piper, Mrs. Best, Miss Holdaway, see you soon."

"But Saben, we can drop Sergeant Colin at the Inn when we see Father."

"No, that's not necessary; it'll be good to stretch my legs," Sergeant Colin said. He gave a nod, then began the short walk to town.

"Now, Piper, you need to hand the dog over to Alberta so we can get her home."

"But . . . ," I stood there with my mouth open as Piper handed me Peachy's lead.

Morvah approached me, put her arm around my shoulders, and walked me to the Model T. "Now do as Saben says; you look exhausted." I lifted Peachy into the back seat. The old bulldog turned around a few times before she curled herself into an exhausted ball. She let out a big sigh and closed her eyes. I shut the door, climbed in front, and didn't say a word.

Morvah and Piper came up to the window. "Thank you for looking out for my granddaughter," Morvah laid her hand, like a benediction, on Piper's head.

I smiled at Piper, letting go of my irritation. "It was my pleasure, and you were such a help with Peachy. You come to Highdrift and visit us anytime."

Saben started the car with a rattle. "I will," Piper said as we slowly pulled away. I looked back, and they both waved. I lifted my own hand just as we turned, and they were lost from sight.

I folded my arms across my chest and sat in brooding silence. Out of the corner of my eye, I could see Saben stealing glances my way. We sat that way until we turned at the old Rowan tree, and I could bear it no longer. "I absolutely do not understand why it was so inconvenient to stop and see Father for a moment. I promised him a visit the minute I got back. I certainly could have driven myself and dropped Piper off. There was no need for you to commandeer and take over everything as usual."

"Now, now, Alberta, let's not say things we'll regret later. I simply did as instructed. I do not doubt your capabilities." Saben pulled up to the walkway at Highdrift. "But I thought you would be pleased." I opened my mouth and was about to start complaining again when I saw a flash of movement. The sun glinted off the front door window as it swung open. Peachy started to bark, and before I knew it, I was in Father's arms, sobbing. I couldn't say anything; I was too choked up. Father handed me his handkerchief, and I dried my tears. Saben stood and smiled, then moved as if to leave. "No, you don't," I croaked and took Saben by the hand and pulled him and Father up the stairs into the house. I sat them down at the dining room table and, of course, prepared tea.

By the time tea was ready, I had composed myself and had a million questions. "Why did the Inspector let you out of jail? Is there new evidence?"

"Not new evidence, just new military service rules. My jailer, Brewster, joined the Navy. He said it was because they changed the rules, and now married men are no longer exempt. I think it was the fact that I finally beat him at chess. Completely demoralized the man."

"Ha, very funny," Saben said. "I'll tell Brewster you said so. But really, the man would have joined up long before this if the Mrs. had let him."

"I know how he feels."

"Now, Father, don't get started on that. We all do what we can. Speaking of doing what we can, Mrs. Brodie requested that I take over Flora Hicks' job curating the pearl donations for this area."

"Hm… I don't care for the sound of that," said Saben. "The more we investigate, the more it appears those pearls are at the core of this. There seem to be two epicenters, London and Lanmorech."

"And I'm plumb in the middle of both." I took a sip of scalding hot tea and set my cup on its saucer with a clatter. I reached across the table for Father's hand. I searched the familiar face and noticed the new fissures down his cheeks and shadows under his eyes. His hair was more gray, and he had lost a prodigious amount of weight. A deep woof came from the front porch, followed by a furious scratching. "Oh, Father, I forgot; I have a surprise for you."

Father held up his hand, "Let me guess. I'd know those dulcet tones anywhere." He patted my hand and scooted back the dining chair. Crossed the floor in a few strides and flung open the front door. "Peachy ma'dear, we are destined to be together," Father said, with laughter in his voice. He squatted down, and the old rheumy-eyed hound licked his face. "Praise be, not even a growl. To what do we owe this tiny miracle?"

"Peachy's welcome? I have no idea what goes on in the mind of an old b..., ugh, dog. As to why she is in Lanmorech, she is a war refugee, like the rest of us. Mrs. Crumpet has taken our advice and gone to stay with her sister. Unfortunately, that had to be 'sans' Peachy. So here she is to keep us company."

"Us?"

I nodded, "I'm staying until this whole mess is put to rest. I'll go up to Penrose as soon as possible and take an inventory of the pearls, then send them up to British Red Cross headquarters with Sergeant Colin."

"That's a good idea; I'll discuss it with the inspector; he wants a look at those pearls as well. Maybe I could go up with you. I can't see why he would balk at such a plan," Saben said.

Piper and Jane

The green Model T purred down the winding driveway flanked by ancient oaks. The trees provided a deep shade but also allowed dappled sunshine to polka dot the roadway. I glanced over at my passenger and smiled. Piper could hardly contain her excitement at going to Penrose House for the first time.

The little girl kept me company since her father, Saben Best, stood me up that morning (on orders from Inspector Blodgett). Saben warned his daughter not to ask too many questions and make a general nuisance of herself, so Piper's little mouth remained clamped shut. But her body bounced, and the child's eyes, behind round metal-rimmed spectacles, opened wider at every turn.

When the car rounded the last bend, and Penrose House came into view, Piper could remain silent no longer. "Oh, my, a castle."

"Well, not quite," I replied. "But it's a grand house, no doubt."

"A grand house," Piper echoed in complete agreement.

I parked the car and gathered up my satchel and purse. My

footsteps crunched in the thick gravel as I walked around and opened the passenger door. Piper hung back; I reached out to help, and Piper gently picked up her little bag and took my hand.

"It looks like Thornfield Hall," Piper whispered as she scooted out of the car and gazed at the massive mansion of gray Cornish stone. The forbidding facade of crenelated battlements did indeed bring to mind Mr. Rochester's country home.

"Who told you about *Jane Eyre*?" I asked.

"No one," answered Piper. I read it myself. It was a most wonderful book. There were many words I didn't understand, but I just looked them up in Grandmother Reed's dictionary. I keep a notebook full of words I look up," Piper said as she hugged her satchel.

"You read *Jane Eyre* all by yourself?"

"Yes, Granny Morvah calls me pre… um, pre."

"Precocious?"

"That's it!" said Piper. "I wrote that in my notebook too. It means 'developing abilities beyond one's years.'"

Piper retook my hand and skipped along happily by my side up the broad stone steps. "Let's go this way," I said, "we can enter the library directly through those French doors."

We walked across the flagstone terrace, and I opened one side of the glass doors and let Piper precede me. "Oh, my," Piper said again as she stood staring at rows upon rows of calf-bound books. "Two levels and a rolling ladder."

"And a spiral staircase," I said. "And oak tables with legs as big as a small tree, big cushy armchairs, and a fireplace."

"Perfect," said Piper. "And the smell; ohhh…I smell leather and wood warmed by sunshine, ink, beeswax, and the lilac scent coming through the open door. Lovely. May I go up the staircase?"

"Of course, you may; just be careful up there."

Piper slowly went up the wrought iron staircase. She stopped every so often to admire the view. Up and up she rose, higher and higher. The next floor was a balcony of bookshelves that ran all around the room. A reading niche with a big soft chair and lamp were on the east wall. Across the room, on the west side, was a window seat with blue velvet curtains and gold-braided tiebacks on either side. Piper stood still in awe.

I called her, "Will you be all right up there for a bit while I get tea?"

A pale little face with owl-like spectacles peered over the ornate wrought iron railing, "Oh yes!"

I walked down the thickly carpeted hall, then across the sizable two-story vestibule where a glorious crystal chandelier dangled. It hung high above a formidable round oak table with feet shaped like eagle talons. I paused to figure out which way to go and spotted the ubiquitous swinging green baize door. I started down the hallway towards the kitchen wing and ran directly into Mrs. Jollie.

"Oh my land, Miss Holdaway, I was just coming to see if there was anything you were wanting," the cook exclaimed as she put her hand to her heart.

"You don't need to do that, Mrs. Jollie; I can fend for myself. Does the staff get a bit of a rest when the family is away?"

"Well, not much really, and this time Dowager Lady Penrose cried off at the last minute, so she's still here."

"Oh, I was going to make tea for two because I brought Morvah Best's little granddaughter with me today. Saben, Constable Best, is picking her up and helping me with the pearls. I thought it would be all right since the family is away."

"That shouldn't be a problem. Lady Penrose will be in her rooms resting, I'm sure. She doesn't go to the library much these days. I'll check with Mrs. Ott and trot over to the library if there is a problem."

"Thank you, Mrs. Jollie; I'd asked Mrs. Ott before, but we assumed all the family would be in London. So best to make sure."

"Come into the kitchen and let's put together a little tea party anyway," said Mrs. Jollie.

I retraced my route back to the library carrying the tea tray with a dizzying array of goodies. I gently slid the tray onto the console table situated strategically outside the library and noticed the heavy mahogany door was slightly ajar. I was sure I had left it tightly closed. I reached out to push the door wide but froze when I heard the quiet hum of voices coming from within. I moved so I could peer into the room through the tiny slit of an opening. At first, I could see no one, but as I scanned the room from my limited viewpoint, I eventually noticed two distinctly different "behinds" sticking out from one of the big overstuffed chairs beside the French doors. The small derriere, which I assumed was Piper's, moved further behind the chair, backed up and turned, then sat on the floor. The much larger "behind" was slower in its movements but followed the same pattern. Next, I was shocked to behold Piper and Dowager Lady Penrose sitting side by side on the library carpet, holding little mewing bundles of fluff.

"That's the kitten you choose?" Lady Penrose said, "I think that's the homeliest of the lot. What about this one? It looks just like Hephzibah."

"No, I want this ugly spotted one. She licked my fingers and bit me."

"Well, that's an odd reason to pick a kitten. I still think you should choose this one; it's much prettier," Lady Penrose insisted.

"No," said Piper, "I want Jane."

"Jane? You have me totally mystified," Lady Penrose said, shaking her head.

"I am naming her after Jane Eyre."

"Jane Eyre!" said Lady Penrose, bending and looking closer at the kitten in Piper's lap. "Well, maybe you're right. She does bring to mind poor Jane." The old lady reached out a finger to stroke the tiny kitten. "Ow, she bit me!"

Piper giggled, "Naughty Jane, but the kitten you have reminds me too much of little Adele."

Lady Penrose lifted her petite ball of fluff and looked searchingly at its face. "Oh, you may be right."

At that point, I thought I should make my presence known, so I rattled the tea tray. Then I pushed open the library door and stuck my head in, "Excuse me, I hope I'm not interrupting."

"Miss Holdaway, look at what this nice lady has given me. I've named her Jane," Piper said as she scrambled up off the floor and ran over to me. She held the squiggling little bundle; the kitten clawed and scratched.

"Here, Piper, not that way," I said, cupping the furry body and gently pushing the kitten toward the little girl. "You need to cuddle her close, so she feels safe and secure, like that." The little cat stopped squirming, and we heard a quiet purr.

"Alberta, come here, gel, and help me up. I'm too old for romping around on the floor. I don't know what's gotten into me." The dowager sat bolt upright on the Aubusson rug, feet sticking straight out in front of her toes pointed directly to the ceiling. I smiled and carried the tea tray to the small table in front of the fireplace. Lady Penrose imperiously raised her arm; I stood and looked at knotted knuckles, the long manicured nails, and thin, blue-veined hands, dumbfounded as to what to do.

"Maybe if you returned to your previous position on hands and knees, I could guide you up onto the settee?"

Beatrice Penrose gave me a baleful look out of her bulging blue eyes. "Maybe I should call Bing," she mumbled to herself. "No, that would be beyond humiliating. I guess I'll do as you suggest." With a groan, the elderly dowager began her contortions. As she crawled on hands and knees towards the tapestry-covered love seat, three little kittens scampered underneath her wavering form. "Shoo, scat, you little devils, shoo," she said. Piper ran forward, dropped onto her knobby knees, and leaned under the wavering Lady Penrose. She scooped up the rampant kittens and sat back on her heels out of harm's way. I grasped Beatrice Penrose by the waist and heaved with all my might. With a whoosh and pirouette, the Lady stood halfway, turned, and collapsed onto the settee. She pulled out her lilac-scented handkerchief and fanned herself. "Oh, my word. At times like these, not that there are many, mind you, I actually miss that ninny Briggs." I poured the exhausted peer a cup of tea and held it out to her. "I don't know if you've heard, but she's disappeared," Lady Penrose said. "Just up and left without a word."

"But I just saw her."

The Dowager had just taken a sip of tea. She inhaled, choked, then gasped for breath. I rushed behind the settee and, remembering my first aid, delivered repeated pounding blows. Finally, Lady Beatrice expelled a bit of air and coughed. Tears ran down her cheeks. She pulled out her handkerchief, between wheezes and gasps, and patted her face, "Oh my." After a few minutes, the elderly woman said, in a shaky voice, "I'll try another drink of tea now." She took an experimental sip. Piper and I watched closely. Suddenly, the dowager burst out, "Drat, that woman!"

I assumed we were talking about poor Miss Briggs again. "I saw her the night before last on the train from London. She was sitting in the Lounge. I didn't have a chance to speak to her."

"How unfortunate; I would like to know what in the world she thinks she is doing. She left without a reference. How does she propose to get a decent post without a recommendation from me?"

"I believe she was contemplating joining the Red Cross as a VAD. She approached Father and me about it."

"Mmm... I see," said Lady Penrose. "Curious behavior, I must say."

The three of us sat for some time, quietly sipping our tea. A discrete tap sounded at the library door, and Saben Best entered, "Am I disturbing you?"

Piper's face lit up, but she remained quiet and ladylike. "Of course not, Constable Best, join us. We are about finished here. However, I have some important business to transact with you before we view the pearls," Lady Penrose said. Saben stood before the Duchess with a confused and wary expression. "You have a very nice child here," she said, nodding at Piper. "I have decided to give her one of Hephzibah's kittens. Piper has made her choice, but they are still too young to leave their mother, so Piper must come and visit Jane often. She may make herself at home here in the library. I will have Bing bring some books down from the nursery wing for her. No twaddle, mind you.

Books my Bertram loved as a child."

"That's very generous of you, Lady Penrose."

"Not at all. I hope Alberta will consent to be my secretary while she is here. She may bring Piper with her when she comes."

I sat dumbfounded but could think of no good reason to refuse, and I now had a reason to be in and out of Penrose House. I smiled and said, "That should be fine for a time."

"Right. Let's look at those pearls. They are in the study safe. Piper, dear, can you give me a hand?" asked Beatrice Penrose. Saben stepped forward to help Lady Penrose, then handed her over to his daughter. Piper reached her arms around the dowager's ample hips, and they made slow progress across the room. Saben raised his eyebrows at me. I shrugged and smiled at the charming picture they made.

As we four entered the study, Lady Penrose pointed Piper towards a metal stand filled with various canes. "Will you be a dear and get me one of those? I still have the collywobbles from that tea." Piper smiled at that. She walked over to the canes and carefully selected an ornately carved, glossy, Rosewood specimen. She gave it to Lady Penrose, who nodded in thanks. The dowager steadied herself and then tapped her way across the gleaming wood floor towards the mahogany desk that dominated the room. She bent over the desk and opened the central drawer, "My, it's dim in here, Alberta; open the drapes... please."

I dragged the heavy wine-red velvet curtains, first to one side, then the next. They made a harsh scraping sound. Light streamed through the French doors illuminating the tiny particles of dust set free by my actions. Lady Penrose frowned in consternation as she rummaged around in the drawer. "Aw, here we are," she held up a small, shiny set of keys and jangled them. Then tapped over to a wall panel edged in wood moulding and swung it open. Behind this was another small door with a lock. Lady Penrose fumbled with the keys and opened the panel. Now we saw the safe itself and the combination lock. "I haven't attempted this for years. Bertram usually opens this." Lady Penrose rubbed her arthritic fingers and flexed them a few times like a real safe-cracker. She twisted the dial to clear the tumblers. "Turn around," she said.

I turned with my hands clasped behind my back and looked out the French doors at a terrace in Italianate style. While my eyes admired the view, my ears strained to listen. There was the well-oiled whir of the dial and then a heavy click of the lever, "Voila!" Lady Penrose stood aside. The safe was about three feet tall and two feet wide and deep. It had three locked strongboxes on the bottom. On top was a stack of three black and white speckled stationer's boxes, all neatly numbered and labeled. On top of these boxes was a notebook. "The notebook is the inventory, and the boxes hold the pearls." You and Constable Best may want to check the inventory, and after that, the pearls are welcome to remain in the safe until they are sent to London."

"Thank you so much. May we set the boxes on the desk and put them away as we inventory?" I asked.

"An admirable plan. I will leave you to it. Piper, shall we go to the nursery and choose some books while your father is occupied?" Lady Penrose held out her hand, Piper grasped it, and they left Saben and me to work.

"Well, Flora was very organized. Everything checks out perfectly," I closed the lid on the last stationer's box, put my hands to the small of my back, and stretched. "I expected the pearls to be from wealthy patrons, but lots of these are from various charity groups and organizations."

"It's nice how many donations have a personal story attached. Miss Hick's did an admirable job of curation," Saben said. "These pearls will make a supreme necklace and be a priceless piece of history."

My eyes swam with tears as I slid the boxes back into the open safe. I blinked to clear them and then double-checked that everything was in its proper place. I bent down to look more closely into the safe and saw threads of dark blue silk protruding from the bottom-most strongbox. The lid itself seemed askew. Just then, footsteps and chatter echoed down the corridor, and Piper burst into the room. She ran to her father and showed him the books she had chosen. Dowager Lady Penrose, leaning on her cane, followed at a more sedate pace. "Thank you so much, Lady Beatrice; we have finished, and all seems to be in admirable order." I reached my hand out and gestured to the safe. "I would, however, like to draw your attention to the condition of this strongbox."

Lady Beatrice tapped over to the safe and peered in. "Most odd, these boxes haven't been opened for years, to my knowledge. They contain the old Penrose family jewelry. The most valuable pieces are in fringed blue velvet bags."

Saben stepped closer, "I don't like the sound of that. I would appreciate it if Lord Penrose took an inventory and let me know if anything is missing."

"He will certainly do that. Thank you, Constable Best," Lady Beatrice said as she snapped the safe shut and carefully spun the dial. She shut the mahogany panel and then crossed to the French doors. She stood with her back to us and looked out at the terraced garden. Piper stepped towards the elderly aristocrat and gently slipped her small warm hand into Lady Beatrice's.

"Daddy says we should be going. Thank you for Jane and the lovely books."

"Oh, my dear, you are more than welcome. But you are to have lunch with me, and then I will have someone see you home." Lady Beatrice turned to Saben. "You and Alberta are not invited. Please escort the gel back to her father."

"May I go to Highdrift and visit Peachy before I come home, Father?"

Saben nodded yes and guided me to the door. We did as we were bid and left Lady Beatrice and Piper chattering like magpies.

The Boathouse

I expected Piper shortly after lunch. It was now three o'clock. Father was out in the backyard working in the orchard, so I stuck my head out the door and called him. "Father, I'm going to run up to Penrose and pick up Piper. I'll be back shortly. Oh, and have you seen Peachy?"

"Hm? Oh, all right dear," came Father's vague reply.

I shook my head and smiled; it was so wonderful to have Father back home. I plucked my raincoat from the hall closet and rushed from the house. White fluffy clouds skittered at a frantic pace across a slate-gray sky. A violent gust of wind buffeted me as I paused to slip on my coat. I fumbled with the Model T's crank and felt a light sprinkling of rain. Morvah had predicted a storm; it seemed she was right.

The car started with a rattle. I backed out of the drive and hummed onto the roadway, which followed the curve of Morwenna Bay towards Penrose House. After wending my way for a mile or so, the rain began in earnest. With each gust of wind, rain-spattered inside the automobile; the front windscreen fogged. I felt in my coat pocket for a hankie and cleared a small space so I could see. I drove for some minutes at top speed before the deluge hit. The Model T plowed through a solid curtain of rain. I stopped the car and grasped the ridiculously inadequate hand wiper. With damp fingers, I flicked the wiper back and forth just as a flash of lightning lit up the countryside in shades of gray, pink, and green. Next came the rumble of thunder. I hoped Piper wasn't out in this storm.

Suddenly Mother Nature decided to take a break. The wind died down, and the rain slowed to a drizzle. After a quick swipe to the windscreen, I put the car in gear and moved the hand throttle. The car inched forward. The road that had been solid hard-pan had turned, in minutes, to a sea of mud. The car slid sideways. Then came another flash of lightning and ear-splitting thunder. A tree on the side of the road exploded and toppled in the automobile's path. I jerked the steering wheel to the right and slammed on the brakes. I avoided the tree, but the Model T slithered off the road into the ditch.

I was halfway between Highdrift and Penrose and dead in the water. I unclenched my hands from the steering wheel. Lord help me, what do I do now? I'd just uttered my plea when a dog's shrill bark echoed in the distance. I clambered out of the car and stepped onto the roadway. My shoes sunk in the mud as I squelched my way to the cliff side. "Peachy, here, girl," I called. The surf murmured in the distance. I peered through rocks and twisted trees, and the curve of the shingle appeared, ringed with kelp. If I leaned way out, the roof of a building was visible. The boathouse must be down there. If Peachy was out in this storm, Piper was probably with her. It made sense that they would seek shelter in the old structure. I'd head down and check.

The path was steep and winding, obliterated in places. Someone long ago had laid stones for makeshift steps, but years of inclement weather had washed and cut away the path leaving small muddied stream beds that were treacherous to navigate. The bushes on both sides of the trail gave an illusion of safety, but halfway down, the bushes ceased, and I faced a sheer drop. I turned sideways and inched my way.

I finally reached the bottom. I bent double, hands on knees, and gasped for breath. A gray, misty expanse confronted me. Only the movement of the white foamy surf as it rolled up the glistening stones delineated the shoreline. "Piper, Peachy?" I bellowed. The answering bark seemed closer this time, but the wind, surf, and screaming gulls made it impossible to be sure.

I pushed wet hair out of my eyes and dabbed my face with my coat sleeve. Then began a long treacherous scramble across barnacled rocks towards the boathouse. Almost at once, my foot slipped sideways, and I lost my balance. I threw my hands out and caught myself before falling flat but lacerated my palms and knees. I lifted the hem of my torn and muddied skirt and saw a red line appearing through my laddered stocking. I cupped my stinging hands around my mouth, "Peachy, Peachy." A dog barked closer at hand. Peachy *was* in the boathouse.

The foundation and lower parts of the structure were square blocks of stone, the upper half, weathered wood. The door and window frames had once been a cheery French blue, but all that remained of the distemper was a few sky-colored flakes and chips. The skeleton of disused window boxes hung off each sill, and a child's broom leaned drunkenly by the weathered blue door.

My knee stung as I limped up the rotten stairs and grabbed the rusty, pitted doorknob. As I twisted the knob, a violent gust of wind blew the door from my grasp. It slammed against the inside wall. My heart pounded so hard I struggled to breathe. Something made me uneasy, and it wasn't the storm. I needed a weapon. I missed my trusty umbrella. The small broom was too light to offer any real protection, but I employed it anyway. I limped to the door and peered in. The room was dark; every window shuttered tight.

"Piper?" I stepped into the hall.

There was another lightning flash; a thunder boom sounded right atop the house. The wind gusted, and the front door blew shut. I froze in the darkness with the child's broom clutched in my hands like a cricket bat, ready to swing. I stepped forward; the vein in my neck pulsed with every heartbeat. Then something skittered across the floor. I let out a startled squeal. An answering growl erupted from somewhere at the rear of the cottage and then came a low sob.

I stopped dead, "Piper? Piper, where are you?" This time a tinkling flash of lightning illuminated a sofa that sat against the boathouse wall to the left; a body lay upon that sofa. I clutched the broom tighter, and the sob came again.

I needed some light. The front door lay within arm's reach. I scrambled for the knob. The light that entered was yellowed and sickly. "Piper?" I said again. My answer was a thump on the door and a paroxysm of growls and barks.

The animal's noise roused the person that lay on the sofa. "All my fault, forgive me, all my fault," the person repeated over and over in a feverish mantra,

I went to the sofa, bent down close to the moaning form, and gasped, "Mrs. Jollie?" Mrs. Jollie acted like an injured animal.

172

She whimpered and shied away from my outstretched hand and soothing voice. "Oh, Mrs. Jollie, what in God's name has happened to you?" I touched her shoulder; the older woman let out a howl of fright and clawed at the back of the sofa. I sat back on my heels and laid my hand on the cushion beside the injured woman. Mrs. Jollie's right eye was swollen shut; the other was tightly closed but twitched and fluttered. A faint line of blood was visible around Mrs. Jollie's nostrils, and her lip was bruised and split.

I stood and put my hand to my mouth, my eyes filled with tears. What should I do? I hated to leave Mrs. Jollie alone. And what about Piper? I looked around the room for a blanket and some water when light footsteps crunched in the gravel outside. I ducked behind the couch; my knees burned, and the child's broom trembled in my hand. Footsteps mounted the stairs and crossed the creaking boathouse floor. I bent down low to peer under the couch and spotted a pair of yellow gumboots. "Piper?" I heard the child's startled intake of breath. "Piper, go back out onto the front porch, now," I commanded in a harsh whisper.

Obediently the little girl did as I told her. I rushed from behind the sofa and followed. I stopped in front of Piper, drew the shaking little girl into my arms, and held her close. We were silent for a moment, and then I squatted down face-to-face with Saben's daughter. "Are you all right?"

Piper nodded but didn't say a word.

"Do you know what happened here?"

Piper shook her head "No," then burrowed herself into my arms again.

"I would like to get you inside and warmed up and dry, but we need some help for Mrs. Jollie."

173

Piper nodded, then took a few hiccoughing breaths. "I was looking for Peachy. She ran away from me when the thunder and lightning started. I followed her here. Peachy ran into the backroom. She scooted under the bed. I couldn't reach her, so I decided to stay here until the storm quit. I went to the other room to light a lamp when I saw Mrs. Jollie lying there. I headed back to Penrose for help; I heard you call and turned around."

"Can you make it up the cliff path, do you think? I left the automobile up there."

Piper wiped her arm across her tear-stained face and sniffed, "I can make it. What should we do about Peachy? May I let her out? She'll be fine as long as the thunder has stopped."

"All right, I'll come with you and check on Mrs. Jollie," I said and held out my hand.

Peachy scratched frantically at the bedroom door. Piper turned the knob and stepped aside. The fat, old, bulldog shot out like a cannonball and scrambled outside. Piper hurried after the dog. I paused to grab the blanket on the metal bed frame and rushed to the front room to cover Mrs. Jollie. "We'll get help and be back as soon as we can," I whispered.

Alberta to the Rescue

The trip back up the cliff seemed to take forever in the foggy drizzle of the early summer storm. We slogged the final fifty feet up the road to the stranded touring car and collapsed on its wide running board. I leaned back against the car door and closed my eyes, trying to catch my breath. Piper sat beside me and attempted to slip off her gumboot. She tugged and pulled, and finally, it came off with a "slurp," taking the child's stocking with it. "Here, let me help you." I took the yellow boot from Piper, dumped the water and fine pieces of gravel, then grabbed the sodden stocking crumpled in the toe. I wrung out the wadded dirty gray cotton, then tugged and pulled to get the sock and boot back on the little girl.

Piper promptly jumped up from the car running board, "We better get going." She grabbed my cold, clammy hand with both of her own and pulled with all her might.

I slowly stood with a groan. "Right, you and Peachy hop in the car. I'll see if I can move her." I walked around front, and gave the car a couple of cranks; it started with a hearty rumble. I clambered in beside Piper, smoothed out the throttle, released the hand brake, put the car in low gear, and tried to move forward. The rear tires spun and slung a wall of mud out the back, the car sunk deeper into the quagmire. I put the car in reverse and increased the throttle slowly. Inch by inch, the green Model T moved backward out of the muddy rut. I turned the steering wheel to the left, gave the car more throttle, and abruptly bumped up out of the ditch onto the muddy road. I kept driving backward until I reached solid ground, then stopped the vehicle.

Piper was jumping up and down on the seat, and Peachy was barking and wagging her tail, "Wee, you did it, Miss Alberta, you did it!"

I sat with my hands clenched on the Model T's steering wheel and smiled at Piper. "Now we need to turn around; that tree is in the road; hang on." I put the car in forward and stayed in low gear.

"Miss Alberta?"

"Yes, dear," I said, never taking my eyes off the slimy roadway.

"Why was Mrs. Jollie in the boathouse? And who would want to hurt her so?"

I didn't know what to say; should I make up some nonsense to soothe Piper's fears? "I wish I knew the answer to either of those questions, but I don't. And I'm not going to fob you off by telling you everything is all right because I want you to be on your guard and refrain from roaming the countryside alone until we get some answers." I took a quick sideways peek at Piper. She sat, head bowed and silent, her left hand absentmindedly stroking Peachy's muddy neck. Peachy's eyes were half-mast in delight.

176

We crept down the road. The Model T bumped over small branches and through deep puddles with ease as long as I kept moving forward. We finally came to the old Rowan tree, which marked my turn for Highdrift. I slowed but did not stop completely, trying to keep my forward momentum. As I took the sharp corner, the automobile fishtailed a bit, but I pressed on. In a few moments, I pulled into the drive. "Father, Father," I called out as I ran up the wide front steps. I opened the front door, "Father?" I looked behind the door at the wooden coat rack. Father's raincoat was gone. "Here, Piper, you and Peachy come in by the fire and get warm." As I walked down the hall, I spotted a note on the console table. The message in Father's bold handwriting said, *"Gone with Saben, back late."*

I shrugged off my wet things and rushed down the hall to the kitchen, where I turned on the teakettle and heated a small pan of milk. I threw some leftover biscuits, cheese, and wizened apples in a basket and filled a vacuum flask with tea. Next, I put a bit of cocoa powder and sugar in the bottom of a mug, added a small amount of boiling water, mixed it smoothly, and then added the hot milk. I took the cocoa out to Piper and a saucer of milk for Peachy. "Now, Piper you and Peachy remain here; I will run into town and get help. My father is with your father; I suppose they are in town."

Piper took the steaming mug of cocoa and took a small sip. "When summer storms kick up, Father's called upon for lots of things, from clearing roads to rescuing sheep. He could be anywhere."

"Hum, well, all I can do is head to town since the road to Penrose House is blocked." I went back into the kitchen, turned everything off, plucked the bag full of foodstuffs from the table, and went down the hall to put on some dry outerwear. "Now you stay here and 'hold the fort' with Peachy." I patted Piper on the shoulder.

Piper ignored me and stepped into the closet, "Granny will help," she said. The little girl pulled out an old red wool pullover. "I can wear this; when we reach Granny Morvah's, I'll get more clothes."

I opened my mouth to argue, thought a minute, and held out my hand. "Let's put Peachy on the back porch with a blanket to keep her out of trouble." A few minutes later, Piper and I were back on Bay Road, headed for town. The rain had stopped, and the air felt cool and moist. "You'll have to direct me, Piper; where does Morvah live?"

"Down on Morwenna Canal, she lives on a narrowboat," Piper stated with pride.

Narrowboat

Piper led me up a well-worn path along a small inlet. I saw a boat maybe six feet wide and quite long, a short distance along the narrow canal. Its glossy navy blue paint with bright yellow trim made a dramatic splash of color on the gray, murky water. The front of the boat closed up tight against the weather, showed no signs of life. However, smoke puffed from the skinny little smokestack that protruded from the snug craft's metal roof.

"Gram, Gram," Piper called as she stepped onto the boat's bow.

Immediately a wooden hatch lifted, two slim doors parted, and there stood Morvah Best silhouetted by lamplight filtering out into the late afternoon gloom. "Piper, what . . . and Alberta, what is wrong?" Morvah reached her arms wide and gathered Piper to her. "Come in, both of you, and get out of this foul weather."

"Piper could use some dry clothes." I stepped into the boat. Its motion threw me off balance for a brief moment, then the craft steadied and felt surprisingly solid. Morvah motioned for me to sit by the tiny coal stove whose isinglass window flickered with a dark orange glow. I sat astonished at the tidy and efficient living space. Gleaming wood walls and a bright tin-tiled ceiling reflected the colorful rag rugs that warmed the waxed wood floor. A delectable aroma emanated from the petite galley kitchen at the center of the boat. It filled the air with the scent of savory herbs, making my stomach growl with forgotten hunger.

As if she could read my mind, Morvah rushed into the kitchen. She plucked a thick earthenware bowl off the shelf, ladled a large dollop of soup, and slid a big spoon into the steaming liquid. As she served me, I explained about Mrs. Jollie. Morvah remained silent. She came to where I sat and flipped up a tiny table. "Eat while we wait for Piper," was all she said, and then she was gone. As I finished the last delectable drop and wished for a piece of bread to wipe up the remaining traces of soup, Piper appeared at my side. She held out a plate of heavy dark bread. I smiled, chose a slice, and ate it in silence.

Morvah bustled into the room again, dressed for the outdoors. She had an oilskin pack filled with first-aid supplies, warm clothes, food, and a canteen. "I think we should take Saben's boat and pick Mrs. Jollie up from the boathouse. There's no way we can get her up that cliff before it gets dark. If the tide's high, we may be able to get very close in."

I held my hand to Morvah and clasped hers, "Thank God you were home."

Morvah nodded her head, "Indeed." The three of us walked by the canal towards Morwenna Bay. The shelter and peace of this place calmed me. The earth and shrubbery surrounding the sodden path seemed to murmur and sigh as the newly fallen rain percolated down, down into the strangely calm bay water below. Hopefully, not just the calm before another storm. "I hope this weather holds awhile," said Morvah, reading my mind again. "I may live on a boat but am not experienced enough to pilot in such bad weather. You perhaps know about boats?"

"Oh, no, I'm afraid that's one thing the Red Cross didn't teach me," I said.

"Da lets me drive sometimes," said Piper as she skipped along between her grandmother and me.

We reached the weathered gray pier and walked down the uneven wood planks. "Tide should be coming back in," Morvah said as she led the way down the rickety ramp to a small boat called, *The Gypsy Piper.*

"Nice name for a boat," I said as I waited for Morvah to climb aboard.

"Da says he named me after the boat," said Piper with a roll of her eyes.

"Fathers will have their little jokes," I said, shaking my head.

Piper nodded in sage agreement as she climbed onto her namesake.

"Hand me down the pack," Morvah called. After a few moments, the motor gurgled and sputtered, then purred to life. "Undo the bow and stern lines," came Morvah's command.

The wind came up, and the boat began to buck like a wild Cornish pony. I just missed being smashed between the side of Saben's boat and the pilings by a hairsbreadth. Nevertheless, I managed to scramble to the bowline, then the stern, and release them both. Piper stowed both lines away and then crouched in the deckhouse doorway to give me plenty of room to jump aboard. Just as I was in mid-air, I heard Morvah gun the engine. I landed on the boat deck in a heap. We were away! I sat on the wet floor to catch my breath and felt the water seep through my raincoat and wool skirt. My hands and knees began to sting from the saltwater.

I stood, keeping my knees flexed, and gained some control over the slap and pounding motions of the *Gypsy Piper* as she pushed her way through the incoming tide and resurging storm. "I'll stay as close to shore as is safe," Morvah yelled above the noise of the small boat's evenly chugging engine. "It will take us about twenty minutes to get near the boathouse at this pace, I would think." Morvah bent down and helped Piper into the pilot's chair, and the three of us looked out the rain-spattered windshield at Morwenna Bay's gray, rolling water. Morvah steered the rollicking vessel with her arms around her granddaughter.

Now, we need to make some plans," I said. "I think we can tie up at the dock and get Mrs. Jollie on board, but should we return to Lanmorech or take her on to Penrose House?"

"That is easily answered," said Morvah. "We take her to Penrose House. Doctor Barnes will be there by the time we arrive."

This took mind reading too far. "How did you know Dr. Barnes would be needed?"

"I can take no credit for that. Saben received an emergency call. Olivia Penrose has gone into labor; it is much too soon. I was preparing my bujo bag of medicinals when you and Piper arrived."

"Fallen trees and mud block the road to the Penrose. How will Saben get through?"

"Saben uses his motorcycle; it can go anywhere. He put the sidecar on and told me he was going to Highdrift for you to ask for your help."

"And I was gone, so Saben took Father. Father left me a note that he and Saben would be late but gave no details."

Morvah reached down and pushed the throttle forward. The engine rumbled even louder than before. The boat sped up and slapped the steel-hard water faster and with more force, again and again. We inched our way along the rocky coast with a redoubled sense of urgency.

The Gypsy Piper

The gray and white seagulls soared in the lofty winds above the *Gypsy Piper*. Behind us, the water roiled and churned; about us, the wind howled; below us, the boat engines throbbed. The instant the boat passed the jutting headland, I spotted the pier and boathouse way down the deserted beach. From this distance, the windows of the structure seemed to flicker with a dim yellow sheen. "It grows shadowed already on the beach. We must hurry. You left a lamp alight for Mrs. Jollie?" Morvah asked.

"No, I did not," I said. Morvah and Piper exchanged looks, then turned as one to look at me. "I don't know," I said, "I have no idea why there should be a light; maybe Saben?"

"I hope," said Morvah with a doubtful shake of her head.

"What if it's the man that hurt Mrs. Jollie?" whispered Piper.

After a moment, Morvah stepped back, "Here, Alberta, take the wheel."

I had no choice; Morvah was gone, down into the cabin. I put my arms around Piper's skinny shoulders and felt the steering wheel vibrate up my arms.

"Just hold it steady; you're doing fine," Piper said as her cold little hands covered mine.

I placed my chin on Piper's shiny brown hair, then kissed where her skimpy braids crisscrossed a ruler-straight part. Thumps and bumps came from below, then Morvah came out, rear first, dragging a yard-long wooden box with rope handles. She knelt and inserted a key in a rusted padlock, lifted the lock off, and laid it on the deck. She raised the lid, reached into the gaping cavity, pulled out a worn canvas bag, and then stood and held it out. "Here," she said. We traded places. I looked down at the greasy sack in my hands and knew what it contained by its dead weight. "Did the Red Cross teach you to use one of those?" Morvah asked as she gazed straight ahead out the rain-spattered windscreen.

I reached into the bag and pulled out the black and glossy .38. My hands shook and felt stiff from the cold as I awkwardly opened the chamber and checked for bullets. "Yes, I can shoot, barely. Do you have ammunition? The gun is empty."

"Look in the box; I'm sure Saben must have bullets for it."

I squatted down and pushed aside life vests, wool blankets, and rope; another canvas bag was in the bottom right corner. "Here we are, Morvah. This must be it." I opened the bag and gingerly reached in to pluck a few ice-cold .38 caliber bullets from their protective nest. I picked up the revolver and steadied myself against the bucking of the *Gypsy Piper*. I slid the bullets into the round chamber with great care, *click, click, click*, and it was loaded. I closed the cylinder. "Done," I said, "Now what?"

"Now Gram and I rescue Mrs. Jollie, and you shoot the man."

"Piper," Morvah said, "the weapon is for our protection only!"

I stood there frozen. The revolver dangled from my hand. I knew enough to keep it pointed at the ground, but I felt my anxiety rise just holding the thing. I looked around for somewhere to set it.

"You'll need to have your hands free when we dock, so put the gun in your bag," Morvah said.

I checked to make sure the safety catch was on, then opened up my pack, which sat on a small bench seat. I placed the gun inside. I sat next to my pack, folded my hands in my lap, leaned back, and closed my eyes. The engine droned on and on as we churned our way. I sat mesmerized until Morvah shifted the boat into low gear. "Alberta, Alberta, I need you to crawl out onto the bow and be ready to jump onto the dock."

I said a quick prayer and opened my eyes. I pulled myself hand over hand along the boat's metal handrail, then stepped up on the narrow ledge. I looked down at the gray churning water, then swiveled and draped my body over the cabin to give myself something solid to cling to. The boat bobbed up and down like a merry-go-round at a carnival. I shuffled my feet side to side and crept along the wet, slick sideboard. I made it onto the bow and climbed on my hands and knees to where the rope lay coiled in a neat spiral. I crouched, grabbed the boat bumpers, tossed them over the side, then held onto the stubby metal bow rail and stood. I planted my feet wide apart, ready to spring as the *Gypsy Piper* glided towards the dock. Closer, closer, I stepped over the boat rail and jumped. I hit the deck in a tangle of rope but managed to stay on my feet. I tugged and pulled as the *Gypsy Piper* danced on the waves; it was like trying to tame a bucking bronco. The engine stopped. I held on with all my strength, and then Morvah was at my side, slinging the rope around the metal boat cleat. I hurried to the stern, Piper slung another line, and the bronco was roped and tied.

Piper handed us our gear, then leaped off the boat. I shouldered my pack, very conscious of the extra weight of the revolver, as the three of us clattered down the rotted wood planks. Our footsteps made hollow thumps, and the weakened structure shimmied up and down. About halfway to the boathouse, Morvah grabbed my arm and motioned for me to stop. The three of us stood still and listened. Waves lapped against the shore, making the shingle of stones clack like castanets. The dock creaked and moaned, and seagulls cried high above, all as it should be. I saw no movement and heard no sounds from the boathouse, but a golden light still glowed through the windows.

"How should we do this?" I asked as I shrugged my pack from my shoulder. I squatted low, unbuckled the leather pack straps, and drew out the revolver. "Do I really need this?" I looked up at Morvah.

"Yes, best be prepared. We should leave our supplies here. Piper, you are to remain until I call for you."

Piper made no protest, just nodded.

Armed and Dangerous

The gun felt like it weighed fifty pounds as Morvah and I crept silently toward the boathouse. My heart hammered so hard I felt lightheaded, and my hands shook as I flicked off the safety catch. The section we first reached was part of the dock and extended over the bay. If we could open the double doors before us, we could float the *Gypsy Piper* inside the garage-like structure.

Morvah reached into her bag, pulled out a nail file, and pried at the rusty metal padlock, which held the weather-beaten doors fast. She wiggled, twisted, and coaxed until she held up a small metal stub. Morvah grunted in frustration and looked around the dock for something else to try.

I turned and walked up the dock to the cottage window and peered in. I could see the whole room except directly below the window where Mrs. Jollie lay. The space was empty. The door to the back room was open, as Piper and I had left it a few hours before.

I returned to Morvah to see how she faired. She shook her head when she saw me, "I cannot budge the darn thing," she whispered.

"You go stand over there," I pointed, "and cover your ears." I went to the doors, aimed the revolver, and squeezed the trigger. The gun went off with a deafening retort, and wood splinters and dirt filled the air. The padlock remained intact, but now there was a gaping hole. The metal latch was gone—the door listed to one side.

"Well, that is one solution. I guess there is no reason to be quiet any longer," Morvah said as she shouldered her way into the boathouse.

As I stooped to pick up my pack, Piper came running down the dock toward me, her eyes wide with fright. "Piper," I called, "everything is fine." She ran to me and buried her face in my skirt, arms tight around my legs. I put my free hand on her shoulder, "I'm so sorry, Piper, it's all right." The little girl stepped back, "I shot the lock off the door." We both looked at the gun in my hand. Piper looked shocked; I felt a bit proud, I must admit.

"Let's go," I said, holding out my hand. Piper and I followed Morvah. The atmosphere in the boat shed was eerie and damp. Every step echoed and threw strange shadows about the walls as we made our way along the narrow catwalks which encircled the black water. A few more steps and we confronted another closed door. Morvah turned to look at me; she raised one raven-black eyebrow and reached her hand out. I clicked on the revolver's safety latch and handed it to her, butt first. She slipped the gun into her shoulder bag and reached for the rusty doorknob. The knob turned freely, and we stepped into the cottage.

189

I half expected Mrs. Jollie to be gone. However, there she was, as we had left her. Morvah rushed over and knelt by the sofa, reached out a gentle hand, and encircled the injured woman's wrist to count the beats that pulsed there. "The pulse is slow; she seems to be sleeping," Morvah said.

I looked about the room, "Someone has been here. There was no fire."

"That must have been the light we saw from the boat," Morvah whispered.

As I searched the room, I noticed a small piece of white paper at the edge of the fireplace. I bent down to pick it up. The paper was a tiny envelope, slightly waxy, a Chemist's envelope. "Morvah, look at this."

Morvah took the envelope from my hand. She licked the tip of her little finger and stuck it in the envelope to pick up a trace of the white grains nestled in the paper's crease. Morvah touched her finger to her tongue, "Morphine." She shook her head, "I don't understand. Someone beats Mrs. Jollie brutally; those contusions are serious, then gives her a dose of medication for pain and lights a fire to keep her warm. Had this person wanted to kill Mrs. Jollie, they certainly could have."

"Mightn't it be more than one person involved?"

"Ah, yes, that would make sense. But why Mrs. Jollie, of all people?" asked Morvah. Just then, the housekeeper moaned.

"I don't know," I whispered, "but we should move the boat into the boathouse, load her on board and get out of here. The sooner we are away from this place, the better I'll feel."

Goolsby's Mother

Getting the *Gypsy Piper* into the boathouse seemed to take forever, but my lapel watch said fifteen minutes. Morvah secured the boat, then headed into the cottage to prepare Mrs. Jollie. I scouted around for something to use as a stretcher. "Here, Piper," I said as I pointed to a pile of junk in the corner of the boat shed, "what about those oars there? They might do for a stretcher with some of that tarpaulin from the boat."

Piper scampered back aboard the moored vessel. She dragged the canvas from under one of the seats. "This might work."

I dug the oars out of the pile, then gathered up the fabric Piper held out to me. "Perfect; it even has reinforced holes around the edges to weave the rope through. There must be a piece large enough somewhere." I helped Piper off the boat, and we searched through the junk pile again. We found a couple of pieces, but none long enough to stretch the length of the oars.

"Miss Alberta, I think there might be some rope in the back bedroom."

"Hmm?" I said as I rummaged on my hands and sore knees

through the pile. "Oh, all right, we should probably see how Morvah's getting along, anyway." I stood, brushed the dust off my blue skirt, and smoothed back the stray tendrils of hair falling about my face. I put my hands at the small of my back and rubbed the tightening muscles. "I really don't see anything long enough here. Let's go." I held out my hand to Piper.

In the cottage, Mrs. Jollie sat on the couch with blankets piled high to improve body warmth. Morvah waived a glass vial of smelling salts under Mrs. Jollie's nose. The pale woman's eyes fluttered. She rolled her head from side to side, "All my fault, all my fault," she moaned over and over.

Morvah reached into her bag and brought out a small bottle of golden liquid. "Mrs. Jollie needs stimulation for shock. I will give her a small sip of my Tuica."

Piper ran across the room to a small cupboard beside the fireplace. She pushed aside the muslin curtain and drew out a tiny teacup. "Here, Gram," she said as she hurried to her grandmother's side, "you may use this."

Morvah smiled at Piper and took the tiny teacup covered in violets. "Thank you, my darling," she said as she poured a drop of her Tuica into the delicate cup and slid her arm behind the moaning woman's shoulders. Then she brought the delicate china teacup, with the drop of Tuica, to Mrs. Jollie's pale lips. "Just a tiny sip Peg," Morvah whispered.

Mrs. Jollie took the tiniest of sips and seemed to hold her breath. Then she swallowed, let out a sigh, and relaxed back against Morvah's shoulder. Tears began to stream down the cook's face.

I walked up to Morvah and touched her on the shoulder. "She looks much better, has some color," I whispered. Morvah nodded her head in agreement. "Piper and I are making a stretcher to get her on the boat."

"That's a good idea; it will be a while before she can walk, and I prefer to leave this place as soon as possible."

Piper grabbed my hand and led me across the bare wooden floor to the back bedroom where Peachy had been trapped a few hours before. "I saw some rope over there," Piper pointed to the other side of the metal bed, "in that closet."

I stepped around the bed and slid back the dirty, rotted curtain to expose a dark and musty closet. A large battered locker lay on the floor, and beside it was a coil of brand-new rope. "What's in the trunk?"

"I don't know; it wasn't here before." Piper knelt before the case." It's locked."

"I think I saw a hammer in the boat shed."

"I know where it is," Piper said. "I'll get it." Piper turned on her heel and hurried out of the room.

I scanned the spartan room as I waited: just the bed and a rickety table under the only window. I walked over and opened the drawer, empty. I moved the window's curtain aside with the tip of my finger, wiped a dirty pane with its edge, and peered outside. Now I had an unobstructed view down the beach. Penrose House was close, just a mile or so around another outcropping of rocks. It shouldn't take long to reach safety once we got Mrs. Jollie aboard the *Gypsy Piper*.

I whirled around as Piper entered the room; she triumphantly brandished a rusty hammer and a tiny pry bar. "I found it, and this thing," she said.

"Smart girl," we went into the closet and knelt on the dirty floor. Piper handed me the tools; the pry bar worked a treat and opened the scuffed brown leather box. I flopped the lid back, and there lay Father's missing books, vestments, and a single collar. Father's collars, always laundered to perfection by Mrs. Pewter, were starched and crisp. This collar hung limp and showed gray on the inner white band. It made my skin crawl to touch it.

"What is it?" asked Piper.

"Just some clothing," I said. I put the collar back and noticed the initials A.H. under the handle. The lid fell closed with a thud. The lock, scratched and bent from my brutal treatment, refused to latch. I lifted the top again and noticed a narrow strap, my Kodak Brownie camera; I moved it aside, and there lay an embossed blue velvet bag. My heart pounded, "We'll just leave it as-is for now." I rose from my knees. My mind whirled, trying to come to terms with this latest development. I entered the front room with the rope. Mrs. Jollie sat limp, leaning back against the couch pillows, eyes still closed.

"Did you find anything?" Morvah said.

"Rope," Piper said, "and a trunk."

"The chest is Father's," I said.

"Oh, Alberta, I'm…" Morvah paused, "how can you be certain?"

"Father's initials are under the handle, and it's full of clerical vestments. But don't misunderstand me. There is no way Father had anything to do with this. The trunk has been missing since we arrived in Lanmorech, proving that someone has been trying to implicate Father. It's the clerical collar. Don't you see? Anyone in a dog collar is a minister."

"That's true," Morvah nodded, "that is what a person would notice." She let out a long sigh, sat very still, and closed her eyes. Suddenly her dark eyes snapped open. "We will take the trunk with us and give it to Saben. He will know what is best to do."

I did not have the same faith in Constable Best. However, I

saw the wisdom in removing evidence of such import.

"All my fault, all my fault," Mrs. Jollie muttered again.

"First, the stretcher." I motioned to Piper to come with me. We returned to the boat shed with the rope. "Now, if we lay these oars like so, side by side, we can lay the tarp over it." Piper drug the heavy canvas over, and we both lifted it on top of the oars.

"It's too big," Piper said.

"Well, we can fold the canvas in half and lay one oar in the crease. First, we need to thread the rope, like this." I knelt on the rough wooden floor, careful of my abraded knees. I laced a length of rough sisal rope through the reinforced holes in the canvas. Piper knelt next to me and uncoiled the rope as I laced. "Now I knot this securely, and we cut off the excess. Now, let's take this contraption and lay it next to the sofa."

"That looks good," Morvah said as we spread our makeshift stretcher on the floor. Morvah leaned close to Mrs. Jollie and spoke softly, "Peg, Peg, we need to move you. Do you understand?" Mrs. Jollie nodded, "Let me help you sit up." Morvah put her arm on Mrs. Jollie's shoulder and guided her upright while I gently slid her legs sideways off the sofa. We had her seated, but her eyes remained clamped shut. "Now, Peg, we will help you to the ground; we need you to lie still on the stretcher. Are you ready?" Morvah helped Mrs. Jollie scoot forward and slide gently to the floor. Mrs. Jollie immediately curled up into a fetal position on her side and began her mantra again, "All my fault, all my fault." I tried to straighten her bent limbs, but she remained rigid. "Can we carry her like this?"

"I can carry her," said a voice from across the room.

Morvah and I gasped and turned. Martin Goolsby stood in the doorway of the boat shed. He walked across the room and scooped Mrs. Jollie up as if she were weightless.

"Let go of her. What do you think you are doing? Put … her … down …" I said as I pummeled Martin's broad back with my fists. "Put her down." It was like hitting a rock. Martin paid no attention to me; he walked out the door into the boat shed.

Morvah and I stood staring at Martin's retreating form, too shocked to move. "Where's the gun?" I whispered to Morvah.

Morvah put a hand to her temple and stood quietly. "I can't think," she said. "I put it in my kit, which is over there," she pointed to the pile of first-aid supplies next to the sofa.

I plucked the revolver from the canvas bag. I left the safety on but gripped it hard with both hands; my knuckles showed white. I pointed it dead ahead and led the way. Morvah and Piper followed close behind me.

Martin stood next to the boat with his back towards us; the injured woman cradled in his arms. He turned around, and his eyes went from my face down to the gun in my hands. "If you shoot, you'll hit my m-mother."

My jaw dropped, I lowered the gun. "Your what, Martin?"

"Peg Jollie is my real m-mum. Now come over and help me get her aboard; I can't do this alone."

I turned my head towards Morvah but kept one eye on Martin. "What should we do?"

Morvah took Piper's hand. "We should get in the boat and take Peg from this young man and get her to Penrose as soon as ever we can. That is most important."

"Well, M-Miss Holdaway?" Martin awaited my decision.

I stood frozen, not knowing what to do. "But how do we know it's safe? We aren't helping Mrs. Jollie if we get her aboard the boat with a murderer."

"I won't get aboard; I will hand her to you and Mrs. Best. Just get M-Mother medical attention."

"Alberta, we must go," Morvah whispered.

I nodded, "Stay behind me, away from Martin," We moved towards the boat in a block, with the gun pointed straight ahead, Morvah and Piper at my back. They clambered aboard The *Gypsy Piper*. I handed the weapon to Morvah, then lifted my leg over the bobbing gunwale.

"Now, what do we do? I can't hold that gun and help with Mrs. Jollie." I knew Morvah was right. She set the gun down on the pilot's seat within easy reach. Martin stepped close and, with extreme care, rested Mrs. Jollie's inert form on the side. Morvah slid her arms under Mrs. Jollie's, and I grasped under her knees. We struggled to lift the elderly woman and lowered her to the boat deck. Mrs. Jollie moaned, "All my fault," and then a fevered, "Martin, Martin," repeatedly. She groped wildly with her hands. Before I knew what had happened, I felt the *Gypsy Piper* heave to one side, and Martin was aboard. I tried to twist around and grab the gun from the pilot's chair, but Martin stood in the way. He glowered at Morvah, and I crouched helpless, at his feet.

"Get out of my way." Martin pushed us aside and effortlessly lifted Mrs. Jollie. He pivoted and took the couple steps into the cabin, and laid his mother on the padded bench, then knelt close beside her. "M-Mother, it's Martin. You're safe now. Don't worry anymore; everything is all right."

I came to my senses and crawled to the pilot's chair. I reached up and felt around for the revolver. The seat was empty. I rocked back on my heels, stumbled back, grabbed Piper, and thrust her behind me, then pushed Piper and Morvah to the stern. The boat gave another sharp heave, and Martin was off the boat, running down the dock back into the cottage.

My ears started to buzz. Giddy with relief, I bent over double to quell the dizziness. Morvah pushed past me. She fumbled with a few knobs until the engine throbbed and roared to life. The bumpers made a complainant squeak, and the diesel engine sent up a plume of foul blue-gray smoke as we reversed out of the boat shed. The *Gypsy Piper* bobbed up and down as we turned. Morvah pushed the throttle full on and headed up the coast to the safety of Penrose House, Saben Best, and Father.

Saben Gets Mad

The veins in Saben's neck bulged. "Mother, what were you thinking? Your actions today have been the most irresponsible ever! Stealing my boat! Stealing my Webley service revolver! Losing my Webley service revolver!"

"Now, Saben, that's not quite true; I took your revolver," I said.

Saben turned towards me, arm raised and shaking his finger. "And you, Alberta, I expect such behavior of my mother, but I thought you had more sense than to go along with such a cockamamie scheme."

"It was *my* idea, don't blame your Mother. How else were we to get Mrs. Jollie out of the cottage?"

"You should have gotten help." Saben was still red in the face, but the veins in his neck relaxed and ceased to pulse.

Piper peered out from behind Morvah's skirt. As Saben noticed his daughter, the veins made a dramatic reappearance. "And to take Piper on this little escapade that I cannot believe!"

Saben stepped over to where his mother stood in front of the roaring fire. "If anything happened to Piper, I would never have forgiven you," Saben said in a harsh whisper.

Morvah looked deep into her son's eyes, "Do you think I would ever forgive myself?"

Piper went to her father and put her arms around his legs. "Da, don't," came her muffled voice. "I found Mrs. Jollie; I wouldn't stay behind. Mrs. Jollie needed help."

Saben, hands on his daughter's skinny shoulders, lovingly traced the top of her tousled braids and gave her a reassuring pat. Over the top of Piper's head, he mouthed the word "Later" to Morvah.

There was a loud thump on the solid oak door of the Penrose study. "If you are finished yelling, Saben," Beatrice Penrose bellowed, "please leave; I need to speak to these two."

Saben gave me a triumphant nod as if to say, "Now you're in for it." He ushered Piper before him out into the hall.

"Well, this is a fine turn of events," Lady Penrose said as she slammed the door. I saw Morvah tense, and I braced for another barrage of vitriol from the dowager duchess. "Because of Olivia's false alarm, I missed all the excitement."

I plopped down on the couch, "Phew, thank goodness. I thought we were in for another scolding."

Lady Penrose wagged her finger at me, "This is a scolding. I thought I was a part of this investigative team."

"There was no time to notify anyone of anything; we were racing against the weather and the tide," Morvah said as she dropped into the high-backed lounge chair beside the fireplace. She leaned back and closed her eyes; one hand went to her forehead.

Lady Beatrice rushed over to a discrete mahogany cabinet

in the corner and lifted its lid; with a rattle, up popped liquor bottles of every shape and color. "No Tuica, but this should do." Lady Beatrice lifted bottle after bottle with her once elegant hands, now knotted and veined with age. She gauged their color, then took a delicate sniff. Finally, she settled on the cut-glass decanter with a chain and metal nameplate. "Aw, here we are. I must confess it has been years since I've played barkeep, but I still can tell the best whiskey of the lot." The elderly Dowager busied herself with crystal glasses. She set three on a silver tray and put a healthy splash of whiskey and a spritz of soda in each. I jumped up and crossed the room to take the tray from Lady Beatrice. "Thank you, my dear; I suppose I mustn't carry this servitude too far." I followed her back to the fireplace. A reflection of orange flame flickered on the gleaming surface of the small tea table as I slid the tray in front of Morvah. Lady Beatrice handed drinks all around, then relaxed against the blue velvet sofa to sip her whiskey and soda.

The three of us sat in silence. I took a sip and felt the sting of the potent liquor. Tears came to my eyes; a warmth burned from my throat to my toes, "Whew," I said.

"Whew, indeed," said Lady Beatrice, as she took another sip, "lovely."

Morvah drained her whiskey and soda in one swallow. "Now, how is Mrs. Jollie, and how is Olivia?"

Lady Beatrice set her empty glass on the tray with a snap. Stood, walked to the fire, and stared into the flames. "Olivia had a false alarm, as I said, and is fine. The doctor says Mrs. Jollie is still in shock, but the bruises are superficial, and she, too, will recover. What I want to know is, what in God's name is going on?"

"We'd all like an answer to that question," said Lord Penrose as he stepped through the French doors on the other side of the study. Lady Beatrice snapped around.

"Amen," said Father as he and Saben entered from the hallway.

"I don't like this one bit," Lord Penrose continued, "Mrs. Ott told me Olivia had a visitor just before she went into labor. A man, from the description, sounds like Martin Goolsby. Saben, I think it is time to apprehend that fellow."

"We can bring him in for questioning, and we will if we can find him. But we can't hold him for the murder of Flora Hicks."

"And why not?" asked Father. "You arrested me."

We know Goolsby and Miss Hicks were acquainted, but we have no proof he was on the train. And . . ." Saben paused and sat down on the window seat; he dropped his head and looked at his clasped hands, "Mrs. Jollie has just confessed."

"What? You have to be kidding! No one in their right mind . . .," chorused the voices of everyone in the room.

Saben held up his hands. "I don't say we believe her, but we need to investigate."

"Mrs. Jollie is Martin Goolsby's real mother," I said.

There was another chorus of "What? You got to be kidding!" This time Saben joined in the protest.

Morvah nodded her head, "That is what Martin Goolsby told us as he helped put Mrs. Jollie on the *Gypsy Piper*."

Saben looked at Lord Penrose, "This is the craziest . . . what next, I wonder?"

"Maybe we should all go home before anything else does happen. Who knows, maybe my turn as prime suspect will come around again," Father said. "It's almost like playing Russian Roulette around here."

It was then I remembered the trunk in the boathouse, the trunk that held Father's Roman collar.

Penrose Pearls

I set my alarm for sunrise the following day placing the old brass clock under my pillow so the noise wouldn't wake Father. I needn't have bothered since the twisting of my nervous stomach kept me from sleeping. I finally gave up, dressed, and sneaked out of the house through the kitchen. I passed Peachy in her makeshift bed. Her bulging eyes tracked my every movement. She lifted her head as I whispered goodbye and silently closed the door. I tiptoed to the old bicycle Father purchased for me at the jumble sale. Its black enamel and chrome shone like new from a recent spit and polish. I grabbed a canvas pack from a hook on the wall and quietly wheeled the Raleigh Roadster out the back and down the walkway.

An early June morning in Cornwall is brisk, and I appreciated my wool jacket and the exertion. The country lane remained rutted from yesterday's storm, but the roadster sped right along. I retraced my path of the previous evening, then veered off onto the nearest side road by the boathouse trail and stashed the bicycle out of sight. I plucked Father's knapsack out of the small wire basket mounted on the handlebars and got an unpleasant whiff of fish as I slid my arms through the canvas straps, then I headed for the cliff.

The sunrise over Morwenna Bay made a glorious display of pinks and oranges. But I didn't dawdle; I just slipped and slithered down the cliff side in dangerous haste. All I could think about was getting this over with, getting home, and having a nice cup of tea. My part in this nightmare would be over. The pearls were already on their way to London, with Sergeant Colin, safe and sound. And as soon as I removed Father's items from the suitcase, there would be nothing to implicate him in Flora's death; he, too, would be safe and sound.

"Brrr," the breeze off the bay cut right through me. I paused to pull my gloves out of my coat pocket. I searched first in one pocket, then the other. All I found was a folded hankie. This wasn't my coat. How could I be so stupid? I searched the pockets again, slipped my hand way, way down to the coat's hem, and felt an envelope. My hand shook as I gently slid the paper out. The address read St. Hugh's Vicarage. My mind went blank for a minute, and a wave of confusion hit me. I put my hand up to my head and got a whiff of that godawful fishy smell that brought Father to mind. I shoved the envelope back into the depths of the coat and hurried on with a new sense of urgency.

I reached the cliff bottom and stopped to watch and listen. There was nothing untoward; I crossed the shingle and entered the boathouse. Rushing to the back bedroom, I opened the closet door and knelt on the dusty wooden floor. The shabby luggage was where I'd left it the day before, hidden under a pile of multi-colored wool blankets on its side in the furthest corner.

I pushed the blankets aside; they tumbled to the floor in a poof of dust and a rainbow of color. My fingers gripped the small trunk's handle and jerked. As I laid the case flat, voices and the crunch of footsteps drifted through the open door. I froze and strained to listen. The sounds came again, louder this time.

I scooted in amongst wool blankets and dusty, forgotten clothes like a child playing an age-old game. The outside noises were muffled, and the pounding of my heart grew louder. With my hand to my chest, I forced myself to breathe deeply. My elbow jostled the clothes, which stirred up more dust. My hand moved from my heart to my nose to stifle a rising sneeze. At the same moment, a scream came from inside the cottage, then a wail, "No, leave me alone! I will not give it to you." The pitch of the woman's voice intensified; "Don't come any closer. Please, Martin, please!" she yelled. Then came the sharp crack of a pistol shot.

I dropped to the floor and felt around in the dark for any solid object. Something cold and metal lay by my hand; I picked it up and crept out of my hiding place. I slid behind the open bedroom door. Mrs. Goolsby's back filled my field of vision; a gun lay slack in her hand. I looked down at the flimsy copper ashtray in my own. Every fiber of my being tensed, then I slung the tray into the living room towards the front door and plugged my ears.

Just as in a bad Penny Dreadful, Mrs. Goolsby spun around and shot at the flying metal disk. The gun continued to click as the hammer fell and the chamber spun. Relieved at the sound of the empty pistol, I looked for something with which to defend myself. Adrenaline pulsed as I crossed over to the rickety table under the window and grabbed the chair. *Bugger silence.* I slammed the door open and crashed into the living room to confront Mrs. Goolsby. I stood a few feet behind her, sucked in my breath, and lifted the chair higher.

"Watch out, M . . . mum, she's behind you," came Martin's familiar stutter. I whirled around. Martin stood leaning against the fireplace.

Anger percolated upwards. I felt my head buzz with it; my muscles tightened; I threw the chair at Martin's head. Martin ducked sideways. The chair glanced off his shoulder, throwing him backward. Next, I lunged and pushed Mrs. Goolsby. It was like beating against Cornish granite; she reached out and grabbed the sleeve of my jacket. I yanked and pulled, emitting frustrated grunts as I forced my way closer to the front door. I dragged Mrs. Goolsby with me, inch by inch. We struggled and tugged; finally, I twisted and let my arms go limp, then shrugged my shoulders to let her pull the coat off completely. Mrs. Goolsby scrambled backward out of control; the wool jacket clutched in her hands. I gasped for breath and turned to run, but Martin blocked the front door. My other option was the boat shed.

I made it inside the shed and slammed the door. The lock was gone (some idiot shot it off), so I scanned the damp, green murkiness for some kind of barricade. On the catwalk lay the unused stretcher Piper and I had made for Mrs. Jollie. I picked it up and shoved it against the door as a brace, ran down to the double doors leading outside, opened them slightly, turned around, plunked myself on the weathered gray deck, and gently slid into the icy water. Clinging to slimy green piling covered with razor-sharp barnacles, I pulled myself under the dock out of sight. The frigid, musty water rocked me up and down, back and forth; I closed my eyes and listened for the pound of footsteps.

Sounds of fury and destruction came from the cottage as the Goolsbys searched. They searched for what I had pressed against my chest in an ornate velvet pouch knotted with a golden cord. With one hand, I fumbled into the inner pocket of Father's fishing vest and took out the royal blue bag I had found in the suitcase. The fabric, embossed with the Penrose crest, enclosed many small, round shapes. This bag had cost Flora Hicks her life, and now it may cost me mine. I took the bag out, slid it between an old beam and the deck floor, and hoped it was safe above the tide.

Minutes passed; I wanted to scream. Finally, heavy footsteps pounded closer, the dock above flexed with each step. "All right, Alberta, I've had enough of this bloody nonsense. Get up here and give me those pearls, or you are d . . . dead. Do you hear me? Dead!" To punctuate his statement, Martin fired a bullet into the dock. The bullet pierced the weathered wood about twenty feet from my hiding place, making an innocent ripple in the briny water. The dock creaked with footsteps and another gunshot, closer this time. Creak, shot, plink, a bullet hit the water ten feet from me. Someone told me once that it was very difficult to shoot anything in the water because water has a surface tension that throws the bullet off its intended path. I prayed they were right.

I put my back against the pilling and held on with one hand, the other hand outstretched before me. I jackknifed my legs and braced them against the post to prepare myself. I waited until the dock creaked again. I took a deep gulp of air and expelled it, then breathed in again, trying to, as Morvah said, "Fill every cell and fiber with life-giving air." I lowered myself into the water and pushed hard off the piling. I kept myself deep; my legs struggled against my skirt and boots. Space and time slowed as I made for the light of the open water. High above, the dock pounded with muffled footsteps. I reached the doorway and had to come up for air. A bullet whizzed past my right ear. I gulped in another breath and dove under again. Fear is a miraculous motivator, but the pulsing adrenaline takes its toll. My limbs felt like lead; my skirt weighed me down. I swam with all my might but made very little progress. I came up for air again. I was outside the boathouse and halfway down the dock.

However, so was Martin, and I was too exhausted to swim further. Martin bent down and reached his hand out; he didn't say a word. I grasped it like a lifeline, which it most assuredly was not. I tried to pull Martin into the water but didn't have the strength.

Martin lifted me out of the bay and roughly dragged me onto the dock. I lay there, beached, gasping for air and dripping wet. "Where's the hoity-toity, vicar's daughter now?" he jeered. I lifted my head; my hair hung down in rattails; I flung it back, out of my way to see Martin. He stood above me, jaws clenched, as he lowered the pistol to his side. He whispered, "I don't want to hurt you, Alberta. You just give me the pearls, and then me and Mum can go away."

"I can't give them to you, Martin. I don't have them."

The dock began its subtle bounce up and down; footsteps approached. "Have you got them?" Mrs. Goolsby asked.

"She doesn't have them."

"Listen, Alberta, all we want is money to get out of here. We don't care about you or your Father. The whole thing got out of our control when Flora was murdered; Martin and I had nothing to do with that."

"Then who . . . ?"

"Give me the pearls, and I'll tell you."

My teeth chattered, and I shook my head.

"Did you search her, Martin?" Martin shook his head no. "You idiot, do I have to do everything?" Martin cringed as Mrs. Goolsby plucked the pistol from his grasp. "Get up, Alberta, go into the back room."

I stood up with exaggerated slowness; water shed from my clothes, and my thoughts raced. What should I do? There was no way anyone would come looking for me. I had to get out of this on my own. So, brilliant thinker that I am, I did what Mrs. Goolsby said. Every step sprayed water ahead of me and made a squelching sound. Slap, slap, slap, I left puddles of water down the dock, through the boathouse, and into the back room. Mrs. Goolsby followed me in and shut the door. She went to the closet, pushed aside the wool blankets, and drug out the battered trunk. "There should be dry stuff in here."

Previously all I saw in the trunk was a jumbled mess of Father's books and clothes. Now I noticed woman's skirts and blouses as well. I slipped off my soaked boots, skirt, and shirtwaist and threw them to Mrs. Goolsby to search. I pulled out the dry skirt, shook it with a snap, stepped in, and pulled it over my wet underthings. Even with hooks and eyes fastened, the skirt slipped from my waist and settled on my hips. The blouse fit the same, two sizes too large and extended in the sleeves. My teeth still chattered, so I grabbed one of the colorful wool blankets off the closet floor and threw it around my shoulders. As I blessed the instant warmth that stilled my shivers, it dawned on me that these clothes were too big to be Flora's. I turned to Mrs. Goolsby, "Whose clothes are these?"

A look of uncertainty crossed the woman's homely features; she didn't answer my question. "You sit and stay put." I lowered myself onto the bed; the bare springs screamed in protest. "If you move, I'll hear you," Mrs. Goolsby warned as she left the room and tugged the warped door shut.

The instant the door closed, I stood; the springs screamed. I froze and listened; a low hum of voices came from the front room. Some of the border pieces to this puzzle were beginning to fit. I needed to hear this conversation to fill in the whole picture. I shuffled to the door and put my ear against the dry, splintered wood. I still couldn't make out the words. The door had no lock; hence, no convenient keyhole to listen through. My only option was to get out. I crossed to the single filthy window and looked the frame over but could see no latch, just two hinges at the top. I pushed the bottom of the frame; the window didn't budge. I dropped the wool blanket to the floor, so my hands were free. I spotted a few nails outside the sill, so I put my forehead to the glass to get a better view. Now I could see down the outside of the cottage.

Through the filthy haze, what looked back at me were a pair of protuberant blue eyes under a glossy thatch of gray hair. I don't know who jumped higher, Lady Beatrice or me. The woman instantly put a finger to her lips and gestured. My heart leaped as I looked and saw Morvah skulking around the corner of the cottage. I strangled a yell and then motioned frantically for the two women to stop. In her infuriating manner, Lady Beatrice gave me the "okay" and followed Morvah out of sight.

I rushed back to the door and opened it a crack. Louise and Martin Goolsby were in the midst of a heated argument.

"I say we just leave. Leave Alberta here."

"She'd never go for that. Alberta has that coat and eventually will figure out the truth."

Martin sat on the sofa and ran his hands through his greasy

hair. "But don't you see we can't hurt Alberta."

Louise Goolsby put her hand to her mouth and turned to look out the window. "Oh God, Martin, why is this happening? Everything I've ever done has been for you. I've loved you like you were my own." Louise Goolsby took two steps forward, "Better even, I'd never give you up."

Martin put his hands over his ears and closed his eyes. He sat like that for a couple of minutes. Suddenly, his eyes flew open and raked the room. They settled on the small wooden piecrust table beside the sofa. He walked over to it and picked up the empty gun.

I bumped the door open and stumbled into the room. Louise Goolsby whipped around. Martin put the pistol down and turned, "Well, Alberta?"

"W-well?" I chattered.

"You heard. Where is Flora's VAD coat? We need that and the pearls."

"You know Martin, you and your mother can have the pearls, but to get them and the coat, you'll have to take me back to Highdrift." I caught a flash of movement in the dusty mirror over the fireplace. I stiffened but rambled on to distract the Goolsby's attention from Lady Beatrice and Morvah. "I um . . . I hid Flora's coat in the Penrose's Model 'T'," I lied. "Let me go now, you can go to Highdrift for the coat, and I will tell Inspector Blodgett who really killed Flora Hicks."

I let my stream of consciousness flow as I watched, in the mirror, the reflection of my two partners in crime sneak by the open front door. "Only one person had ample opportunity to access the safe at Penrose. One person that made sure Beatrice Penrose discovered Flora's body at the church auction. One person that searched Highdrift well before anyone else knew about Flora's coat. One person always on the periphery but never a central figure. It dawned on me when I saw my camera in the suitcase and the clothes that were two sizes too large. She has been at least one step ahead of me the whole time, and she's been one step ahead of you, too. Mary Briggs hid the pearls in that old case in the backroom. They've been there all along until I took them and hid them under the boathouse dock."

"The dock?" Louise Goolsby and Martin forgot all about me in their scramble to get out into the boathouse and search for the pearls.

I twirled around and sprinted to the front door, "Go away!" I hissed at Lady Beatrice and Morvah. I noticed, too late, how stiff and wide-eyed the two ladies were. They stood shoulder to shoulder. I reached and pushed them aside and found myself staring at the cold blue steel of Saben's Webley. I let my hands fall, backed up to the porch rail, and slithered down to the floor, my energy gone.

"Very smart, Alberta," Mary Briggs said. "But too late." Mary motioned with the gun for Lady Beatrice and Morvah to precede her into the boathouse.

Father to the Rescue

Mary Briggs was right to ignore me and leave me slumped on the porch. I was no threat to anyone—least of all Miss Briggs with twenty pounds on me and a gun. I closed my eyes, just for a minute. In the wind, I heard my name. It took all my will to open my eyes. First, I could see nothing. Then, down the beach, stumbling off the cliff path, I saw a man brandishing an umbrella. He yelled my name, "Alberta, Alberta!" Beside him ran a small white dog.

My wool blanket fell to the porch as I stumbled down the steps and across the sand. I had to stop Father. The jagged barnacle-covered rocks sliced at my feet, bringing me to a halt. I waved my arms like a mad thing. Within minutes, Father reached me, and I was in his embrace, "Alberta, dear."

"Father, you must go at once and get help; there's nothing you can do here."

"Ah, you underestimate your Father, sweetheart. Saben is on his way by boat and will be here shortly. Peachy and I are the diversion."

"But it's too dangerous. Lady Beatrice and Morvah are in there, the Goolsbys are desperate, and Mary Briggs has a gun."

Father's face suffused with red, and a vein pounded at his throat. He grabbed my shoulders, gently but firmly set me aside, and headed for the boathouse. I heard him clear his throat and begin a rousing version of *Onward Christian Soldiers*. I've never been so proud. I ran to him, slipped my arm through his, and joined the cacophony. Peachy hopped and skipped beside us, barking with excitement. Together we marched up the cottage steps, ready to face our foes. We stopped short; the room was empty. Splashes, footsteps, and voices raised in argument echoed from the boat shed. I shook Father's arm, pointed to the piecrust table, and motioned for him to pick up the empty gun.

As Father turned, Peachy lifted her head, her nostrils twitched, and a low growl rumbled in her chest. Peachy's bulging eyes widened, and she took off like a bullet across the room, nails making a loud *scritch-scratch* across the wood floor. I lunged for the aggravated canine, but she evaded my grasp and began to bark. I caught Father's eye, "Should I warn Martin?" Father shook his head with a slight smile and handed me the pistol. We walked to the boathouse door. Peachy clattered across the dock and clamped on Mary Briggs's ugly black skirt.

Mary's face paled as if she'd seen a ghost. She kicked at the portly pug-faced dog and screamed, "Martin, Martin!" She tugged at her skirt and almost dropped her gun in panic. "Louise, your idiot son!" Briggs ranted as she dragged the obstinate bulldog across the dock. "Your idiot son didn't kill this damnable dog; look, look," she raved. Then, her face purple and hands shaking in rage, she pointed the pistol at Peachy.

214

Martin had just climbed out of the water. He stood hunched over, water cascading off his clothes, gasping for breath. He held up the dripping blue velvet bag of pearls in triumph. Then saw the gun pointed at Peachy. With a roar, Martin ran for the pistol and Mary Briggs. The crazed woman turned and fired. Martin stopped, a look of astonishment on his face. He put his hand to his side; blood began to seep through his fingers. "Mother," he said and collapsed.

I broke out in a cold sweat; the room began to spin. "Alberta, Alberta!" I heard a voice say. Then I felt the sting of a sharp slap on my face. My head snapped back; Morvah was in front of me. "Alberta, get a cloth to staunch Martin's bleeding."

I put my hands to my head and stumbled past Mary Briggs knocking her out of the way. "Stop, Alberta! Everyone stay where you are," she screeched, totally out of control.

I ignored the crazed woman and made it to the kitchen. I leaned on the counter, took a couple of gulps of air, and then rummaged in drawers until I found some clean cotton towels. I got one wet at the sink pump and rushed back through the cottage. I brushed past Miss Briggs and gave her a shove. "Get out of my way," I growled and knelt by Martin. Morvah had already opened his shirt. My hands shook as I patted the wound with the damp towel and then laid on a dry cloth.

"You look worse than I feel, Alberta," Martin whispered. "My side burns a bit, that's all." Martin laid his head back and closed his eyes.

"Martin is going into shock. We better get these wet clothes off him and cover him with blankets," I said. Louise Goolsby rushed over. "Let me help, please," she sobbed.

"Silly fool, why'd he have to go and interfere? Now you women move aside, give me those pearls." Mary Briggs rushed forward.

"Oh no, you don't," Lady Beatrice said as she grabbed her secretary's arm.

"Let go of me, you old battle-ax," Mary Briggs yelled as she shoved Lady Penrose onto the rough wooden dock.

"Here now, that's enough of that!" Father said, letting go of Peachy. Peachy charged ahead and clamped on Miss Brigg's ankle. At the same time, Father brought down the trusty steel umbrella "smack" with a sharp chop on the secretary's gun arm. The revolver dropped to the floor and skittered across the dock toward me. I grabbed the gun. I passed it to Lady Beatrice, who gave the pistol a hefty push and consigned it into the murky green depths of Morwenna Bay.

Mary Briggs let out an elemental howl, "You . . ." she screamed, fingers outstretched like claws. Peachy bit deeper into the fatty flesh of the woman's calf, "Ugh," Miss Briggs collapsed in a heap.

"Peachy heel!" quivered Lady Beatrice's commanding voice.

Peachy let go. On stubby bowlegs, square head held high, the old dog waddled over to Martin Goolsby and lay gently beside him.

Just like that, the nightmare ended. Saben and Sergeant Colin came to our belated rescue in the *Gypsy Piper*. The two officers stepped onto the boathouse dock to behold Lady Penrose holding her former secretary, Miss Mary Briggs, at gunpoint. Martin Goolsby, wrapped in wool blankets like a mummy, lay propped up against an old lifeboat, Peachy at his side and Louise Goolsby seated atypically silent, tears running down her cheeks.

Father and I gathered around Morvah, who had the priceless string of Penrose Pearls dangling from her long shapely fingers. "It's about time you showed up, my darling," Morvah said.

"We had to drop Dr. Beagle off at Penrose. Olivia is in labor, the real thing this time."

Sergeant Colin went over to Beatrice Penrose and reached for the pistol, "Mam?" he said.

Lady Beatrice handed him the empty gun and nodded toward Mary Briggs. "Keep a close watch on this woman, Sergeant; don't trust her for an instant."

Father escorted Morvah and Lady Beatrice out of the cottage. He returned a moment later, "I forgot the pup. Peachy girl," he called. Peachy rolled her eyes and stayed put.

Lady Penrose stuck her head back in the room, "PEACHY, COME!" The two old women, peer of the realm and pudgy dog, left the boathouse. We heard Lady Beatrice admonishing Father as she stepped down the stairs, "You must be in command, be firm, Ambrose."

Sergeant Colin bent over Mary Briggs, "Get up, please, Mam."

"I can't, you idiot. Can't you see I'm injured?" Mary Briggs shrieked.

Sergeant Colin lifted his head; his eyes met mine. "Sprained and bruised right arm, dog bite right calf," I explained.

"That dog should be destroyed; mean, vicious, little . . ." Miss Briggs said.

Martin murmured under his breath, "Peachy deserves a medal."

Fini

Saint Tancred's was full to overflowing. Every citizen of Lanmorech was in attendance to witness the baptism of the future Lord Penrose.

I buried my face in the yards of fine linen and lace as I cradled Albert Ambrose Bertram Penrose in my arms. A tear of pride and happiness rolled down my cheek.

Lady Beatrice proffered her lavender-scented hankie. "Here, Alberta, you may as well keep this."

"Ha, thank you, I think I will," I said.

Saben reached around me and plucked the wavering handkerchief from the dowager, "Wouldn't want Alberta to drop the lord and heir." He patted my cheek with the delicate lawn and smiled into my misty eyes.

My face burned under his scrutiny. I dropped my head again, and Saben whispered, "You look beautiful, Alberta."

My heart began to pound, and I was grateful for the commencement of Father's stentorian tones. "My dear brothers and sisters in Christ, it is my honor to officiate at St. Tancred's for this blessed event; the entrance of Albert Penrose into God's community of faith through the holy sacrament of baptism." Father stood resplendent in snow-white vestments and raised his arms to encompass the smiling crowd. "Welcome to each and every one of you. I hope for these few moments, we can live in the present and not be weighed down by the cares and worries of the future. I must confess my delight in this day is partially selfish; for this perfect child, this gift from God, is my namesake, and my daughter is to be his godmother."

Saben put his arm around me and guided me up the church aisle to the baptismal font in front of the altar. The Penrose family filed in behind us; baby Albert began to squirm in my arms. I pushed the scratchy lace away from his face, then rocked and soothed him. I kissed his cheek, and he grabbed a lock of my hair and clutched it in his tiny, perfect fist. That settled him, and I gave my full attention to the service. I'd witnessed baptisms hundreds of times but never one so poignant. I struggled to keep my composure and could barely choke out my responses.

When Father sprinkled Holy Water on baby Albert's head, the child didn't utter a sound, but an expression of infinite surprise flitted across his perfect features, and he clutched my hair all the tighter.

After the benediction, we sang and filed out of the church into the bright August sunshine and made a receiving line so everyone could have a quick peek at the newest member of the congregation of Saint Tancred's.

Then Lady Beatrice swooped down, "You've had my angel long enough, Alberta." The dowager plucked Albert from my arms and clutched him to her ample bosom.

"Don't smother him, Mother," Bertram Penrose said as his mother whisked her grandson away.

There was a butterfly-light tug at my skirt. "Miss Alberta," Piper said, "that was a beautiful service. May we get some cake now?"

Saben chuckled and grabbed his daughter's hand. "Lead the way." Piper placed her warm palm in mine, and the three of us strolled over to the long cloth-covered tables on the lawn under a striped marquee. "Why don't you and Piper grab a table, and I'll get the refreshments?"

"How about that table over there by Sergeant Colin," Piper said. Before I could stop her, Piper ran to greet the policeman.

"Hello, Miss Piper, Miss Alberta," Sergeant Colin said with a polite nod of his head. "I'm happy to see you ladies again."

"Sergeant Colin, what a surprise," I said as I took my seat. "I, too, am glad. Thank you for taking care of the pearls and delivering them without incident to Mrs. Brodie at Red Cross headquarters; and for coming to our rescue at the boathouse."

"Oh, Miss Holdaway," Sergeant Colin said with a twinkle in his eyes and a shake of his head, "I wouldn't have missed that for the world."

Just then, Saben approached with a tray of cake, tea, and lemonade. As he slid the tray on the table, Sergeant Colin stood with a big grin and held out his hand. Saben took it, and the two men shook hands and chuckled like a couple of schoolboys.

Piper looked at the two men, then at Alberta. I shook my head and shrugged. "Saben, what are you and Sergeant Colin laughing about?"

"Oh, we had quite a time with Miss Briggs; we both have the scratches to prove it. We took her into the station where she received medical attention, and then she confessed to everything."

"Yeah," said Sergeant Colin, "she just broke down and told us how she hatched the whole plot when she heard about the pearls and met poor Flora Hicks. Mary Briggs orchestrated it all and used Martin and Marian Goolsby to carry out her scheme."

"But why," I asked.

"Solely for money," said Saben. "She needed the money to get out from under Lady Beatrice's thumb."

"When Mary Briggs stopped by Highdrift with Mrs. Jollie, she rambled on quite a bit about wanting a home of her own. She seemed quite fixated on the idea."

"Mmm, that makes sense," said Sergeant Colin, "she had a rough and meager upbringing. She received her secretarial training through some charity or other."

"And she is highly intelligent and capable; no one lasts in Lady Penrose's employment that isn't exceptional," said Saben.

I took a sip of my tea, then set my teacup on its saucer with a clatter, "Why involve Father?"

Saben and Sergeant Colin looked at one another. "Well," said Saben, "as near as we can figure, Mary heard about your father's troubles through gossip below stairs at Penrose House."

"And then, when she saw Lord Penrose and Vicar Holdaway having a drink on the *Night Riviera,* she realized your father made the perfect scapegoat," finished Sergeant Colin.

"How cruel to implicate an innocent man already in a pit of despair."

"And diabolical," Saben said, "to turn your black coat around and have your white-collar showing. All Mary Briggs had to do was keep in the shadows with her head down and make sure the waitress, having a surreptitious smoke at the back of the train, got a quick glimpse."

"So we had an eyewitness," said Sergeant Colin. "Very convenient."

"If that hadn't worked, I'm sure she would have thought of something else equally nasty," I said with a quiver in my voice.

Piper patted my hand," Don't worry, Miss Alberta; Father will take care of you."

Saben choked on his tea, and Sergeant Colin threw back his head and laughed. My cheeks burned, but I couldn't resist giving Saben a sideways glance. He looked stricken; he just sat there with his mouth open.

"Well, since Saben doesn't look too enthused, I'd be happy to be of service. I shall be spending some time in London at the Red Cross headquarters. I hope I shall see you there."

I took another sip of tea to compose myself. "Oh, um, I'm sorry, Sergeant Colin, but Mrs. Brodie has asked me to do fundraising and first-aid classes for the Red Cross here in Lanmorech. Father and I are staying at Highdrift."

"Oh, that's too bad; I mean not bad; it's good that you are keeping out of London," Sergeant Colin stammered. "The Germans have stepped up their incendiary bombing."

"I know, and it worries me that Mrs. Pewter and Nancy are in the thick of it. I leaned forward in my chair, "Can I ask you a favor, Sergeant?"

"Of course, Alberta, err . . . Miss Holdaway, anything."

"Could you check on Mrs. Pewter and Nancy from time to time? Father and I are trying to persuade them to relocate but to no avail." Just then, I felt a familiar squeeze on my shoulder.

"What's this about Mrs. Pewter?" Father said.

"I asked Sergeant Colin to check on her when he is in London. She took quite a shine to him."

"You mean Nancy did. She does appreciate a handsome man." Father laughed.

Now it was Sergeant Colin's turn to get red in the face.

Suddenly Saben jumped up from his seat, "Alberta, could I speak with you for a moment?" Saben held out his hand.

I nodded and scooted back in my chair. "What's this all about?"

"I just need your advice about something." Saben nodded to Father and Sergeant Colin, "Please excuse us."

"May I come too, Father?" Piper asked.

Saben put his hand on Piper's head, "Not just yet, sweetheart; I need to speak to Alberta in private. As soon as I get back, we'll go see Grandma." Everyone at the table looked as surprised and confused as I was, but I let Saben lead me away.

Saben put my arm through his. We took the path that wound through the trees, then to the shore of Morwenna Bay. The two of us stood silent and still, mesmerized by the glorious golden sands and turquoise surf of the Cornish seaside and the tension between us. A tension that pulled us close but also kept us apart. Did Saben feel it too? My heart beat faster. I bent down, pretending intense interest in a scallop shell, which lay at my feet half-buried in the warm buff sand.

I stood, and Saben stepped behind me and put his hands on my shoulders. "Alberta, I have something to ask and to tell you."

The warmth of Saben's hands on my shoulders made me dizzy. I leaned against him and decided to say yes when he asked me to marry him.

Saben turned me around to face him. "Alberta, I am going away. The Admiralty is sending me to France."

I gasped; my shock must have shown on my face because Saben gathered me in his arms. "It's only for a short while, I

223

hope, but I'm worried about Piper."

I pulled away and nodded, "Of course, of course," I said as I felt in my pocket for Beatrice Penrose's hankie. I patted my eyes before the tears that stung fell and betrayed just how upset I was. "Father, Peachy, and I love Piper and would do anything for her."

Saben searched my face, "You really do, don't you?"

I nodded again, "Is that so strange?" I stared him straight in the eyes. We stood like that for a minute, then I pivoted and took a few halting steps in the sand.

Saben grabbed my hand, but I kept on walking. "Alberta . . . wait . . . Alberta," Saben fell in step beside me. "How well do you know that guy?"

I kept walking, "I have no idea who you are referring to."

"Sergeant Colin, you two seem awfully chummy."

"I am not chummy with him . . . yet, but would it matter if I was?"

Saben stopped. "Yet . . . what do you mean, yet?"

I just kept plowing through the golden Cornish sand, glad Saben could not see the satisfied smile on my face and the hope in my eyes.

Afterword

I relied heavily upon the lovely autobiographical, *Home Fires Burning, The Great War Diaries of Georgina Lee,* for the flavor of life in England during the First World War. Georgina's only child, Harry, had been sent to the country for safety, and these are the diaries she wrote to her son throughout the war.

This is a work of fiction; any mistakes are my own. I did alter the timeline for the Red Cross Pearl Drive to better fit my narrative, but it did occur at the end of the war. Funds went mainly for the rehabilitation of returning soldiers. The *Night Riviera* is a real sleeper train that still runs between London and Cornwall.

Thank you so much for reading. It would mean so much to me if you would leave a review on Amazon and Goodreads. You can't believe how important that is! Let me know what you enjoyed most, and watch for my new mystery, *The Mermaid Pool.*

Made in United States
Orlando, FL
04 September 2023

36680122R10140